GENTLEMEN PREFER HEIRESSES

By Lorraine Heath

GENTLEMEN
PREFER
HEIRESSES

LORRAINE HEATH

AVONIMPULSE
An Imprint of HarperCollinsPublishers

GENTLEMEN PREFER HEIRESSES. Copyright © 2017 by Jan Nowasky. All rights reserved. Printed in the United States of America. No part of this book may be used or reproduced in any manner whatsoever without written permission except in the case of brief quotations embodied in critical articles and reviews. For information, address HarperCollins Publishers, 195 Broadway, New York, NY 10007.

Digital Edition AUGUST 2017 ISBN: 978-0-06-268124-9
Print Edition ISBN: 978-0-06-268125-6

Cover art by Anna Kmet

Avon Impulse and the Avon Impulse logo are registered trademarks of HarperCollins Publishers in the United States of America.

Avon and HarperCollins are registered trademarks of HarperCollins Publishers in the United States of America and other countries.

FIRST EDITION

17 18 19 20 21   OPM   10 9 8 7 6 5 4

For all the lovely readers

From the Journal of Lord Andrew Mabry

I was born the spare. The second son. The extra. The one held in reserve. The one who arrived without fanfare or bells tolling. The one who would not inherit unless the heir cocked up his toes.

Since my older brother was a most sensible man, his demise was unlikely to take place before he provided his own heir and spare.

So little was expected of me.

I was to be a gentleman, to play, to squander my allowance, to provide entertainment, to be always pleasant and always in the background. I embraced these duties as though Great Britain would fall if I did not see to them with enthusiasm and diligence.

I was a right jolly fellow, with no plans to ever marry. After all, I was not responsible for the next generation. A wife would hinder my pleasures, would be a symbol of the responsibility I was allowed to avoid. I was carefree. I wanted to remain that way, had taken a vow to welcome death in my old age as a bachelor.

Then I met her.

And she challenged everything I knew and understood about myself.

Chapter 1

As organ music wafted up to the church rafters, Miss Virginia Hammersley strolled slowly down the aisle toward the altar where the Marquess of Rexton stood tall and handsome. Gina was the one who was supposed to marry this Season, the one whom the marquess had supposedly been courting.

Yet today she was serving merely as the maid of honor because the Marquess of Rexton had fallen in love with her older and incredibly scandalous sister. Since the *beau monde* loved scandal and the marquess's family equally, the pews were fairly packed. Amazing how love could right a ruined reputation. She took quite a bit of pride in her role of seeing it righted, of seeing Tillie—if not fully embraced by Society—at least no longer being shunned by it.

As Gina neared, Rex acknowledged her with a slight bowing of his head and a smile that spoke a volume of happiness, the sort of smile she dreamed the man she eventually married would direct her way. One that foretold a love so grand that time would be powerless to erase it. Adoration that could not be measured. Esteem that knew no bounds.

Emotions exemplified in every romantic novel she'd read and clutched to her bosom when finished, tears rolling down her cheeks. Such affection could not be written about if it didn't exist. She was determined to find it in the form of a duke, or a marquess, or an earl. She was one of the wealthiest heiresses to ever set foot on England's shores. With her sister's redemption, the possibilities for Gina's own future and acquiring all she held dear opened up dramatically.

While the Season was nearing its end, it was not yet over, and she was determined to make the most of the time that remained, so she would be taking this same journey as a bride before year's end.

Only after she took her place did she dare glance over at the man standing beside the marquess—his younger brother, Lord Andrew Mabry. Or she'd intended to merely glance over, but his gaze captured and held hers as effectively as if he'd secured it with rope and locked it behind bars. From the moment she'd met him one night at the theater in May, she'd had a difficult time breaking eye contact with him once it was made. Like his brother's, his eyes were blue but there was a stormy quality to them as though he relished flirting with danger, with impropriety. Rumor had it that he'd recently been involved with an actress. Common knowledge was that he never intended to marry, which made mothers wary of him and young girls heed the warnings to steer clear of him.

Not that she needed any warnings. He made her insides feel funny, her skin warm, her toes curl, her nerve endings tingle—and all of that was with a few feet separating them.

Besides she had her heart set on marrying a titled gentleman. Pity, for Lord Andrew to become titled Gina's sister would have to become a sonless widow. Tillie had experienced too many unhappy years for Gina to wish such a dreadful outcome on her.

Still she couldn't deny something about Lord Andrew called to the wanton in her, especially when his perusal was as leisurely as it was now, and she could imagine that in his mind he was slowly unfastening each button, giving laces their freedom, easing her gown off her shoulders, tugging it down until her breasts sprung free and that luscious wicked looking mouth of his could close around a pearled nipple. She knew it would be pearled because they always puckered when he was near, when his gaze dipped, leaving her with the impression he knew precisely what she looked like beneath her clothing.

Mendelssohn's "Wedding March" suddenly burst forth in a crescendo from the organ, breaking the sensual spell into which she'd fallen. Grateful for the excuse to turn her attention to the back of the church, she watched as her uncle led her sister in her lovely lilac gown—white being forbidden since it wasn't her first marriage—up the aisle. At that moment, she missed her parents more than she thought possible. Her mother had passed a few years earlier, her father a little over a year ago. With his death, she and Tillie had acquired a fortune, would continue to receive an annual income from her family's firearms company. It was the reason she could fairly dictate whom she would marry. It gave her power. She could even set her sights on a prince if she so desired. Perhaps she would.

Tillie was marrying a marquess who would one day inherit a dukedom. Her sister would become a duchess. Gina thought it would be grand to acquire that rank as well. Sister duchesses—what fun that would be. Although truth be told, she'd settle for a pauper if he caused her to radiate as much happiness as Tillie did now, gliding toward her.

Her sister deserved this joy. Her first marriage had resulted in a scandalous divorce that had seen her tossed out on her ear by the aristocracy. Gina had no doubt this marriage would last until the end of time.

The love with which Rexton gazed at his bride as she took her place beside him no doubt had every woman within the church sighing with longing for the same sort of adoration to be cast her way. Gina certainly did.

She wanted what Tillie had, was determined to acquire it.

Family obligation and love for his brother kept Lord Andrew Mabry—the ducal spare—tethered to the altar when he'd rather be anywhere else. Wedding ceremonies were so blasted boring, seemed to go on forever, and had no luck holding his attention.

Miss Virginia Hammersley on the other hand—

He was struggling to ignore her, to not be caught staring at her while envisioning all the lovely alabaster and pink skin that existed beneath the white gown decorated in pearls. His thoughts were entirely inappropriate, and he knew if Rex discerned their direction that at the end of this torturous ceremony Andrew would be fending off his brother's fists. The marquess was incredibly protective of Gina, had been striving to assist her in finding a husband—until he'd fallen head over heels in love with her sister.

Andrew was a great believer in love. How could one not be when raised by parents who adored each other? Still, he thought it a waste to focus all the emotion on one person. He preferred to spread it around. Recently he'd fancied an actress, before her a shop clerk, before that a barmaid, an artist, a writer, a harpist, and a coalminer's daughter. She'd been his first. He couldn't smell coal burning without thinking of her fondly.

But then he thought of them all fondly, always ended things on good terms. Well, almost always. There was one exception that he tried very hard not to remember.

Gina Hammersley was different. Different from the others. Different from anyone he'd ever known. He couldn't quite figure out why. Perhaps because she was forbidden, untouchable, the sort of woman with whom a man didn't dally. Sterling reputation, scandal free, destined for the altar. A lass who would cling to her virginity until her wedding night. Not the kind he was at all interested in getting to know.

Still, he surreptitiously slid his gaze over to her. She was an elfin thing, petite, delicate. She watched the couple exchanging vows as though she'd never seen or heard anything so wonderful in her entire life. He had an insane urge to show her something far more marvelous: the world from atop a mountain, a slow journey down the Nile, pyramids, the Taj Majal, Paris, Rome. A kiss. A touch. Pleasure. The possibilities began spinning through his mind, as he imagined her looking up at him with the adoration she now bestowed upon his brother and his bride.

But he knew the truth of her: she was for only fantasies and dreams. She desired rank and title. He was merely the spare. While she might intrigue him, she was a challenge he could not accept.

A somewhat quiet yet intense throat clearing jerked him from his reverie, and he found himself gazing into eyes very similar to his, issuing a rebuke, revealing a bit of impatience. Right. The ring. He dug it out of his waistcoat pocket and dropped it into his brother's waiting palm. As Rex turned away, Andrew was left with the distinct impression the marquess was aware of the direction his thoughts had wandered, in which case he'd no doubt receive a lecture following the breakfast celebration. Not that he'd pay it much heed.

He shifted his attention back to Miss Hammersley. Tears were welling in her eyes. Why the deuce did women weep at moments such as this, when a man was being shackled for life? It should be the man crying, because all the joy was going to be drained from his life.

CHAPTER 2

"You're to stay away from Gina."

Standing in a far corner of the terrace, sipping scotch as darkness descended, Andrew didn't even bother to glance over at his brother. "Shouldn't you be off bedding your wife by now?"

The day had been infernally long. The wedding *breakfast*—he didn't know why it was labeled as such when it had occurred in early afternoon—had gone on forever. Following that, a host of young ladies had demonstrated their mastery of the pianoforte. Although for some, mastery was a generous over-statement. And now a ball was underway, with no plans for it to come to an end until midnight. If he were to slip away for more entertaining endeavors would his absence be noted?

"Tillie is changing into her traveling attire as we speak. We're going to Kingsbrook Park for a few days." Rexton raised horses at his personal estate. Both he and his now-wife were mad about equines and racing. "While we're away you're to avoid Gina."

"I don't require a warning. I have no interest in the girl."

"That's untrue. I've seen the way you've been looking at her all day."

After tossing back what remained of his scotch, Andrew faced his brother. "What was I supposed to do when the entire day has been naught but shoving her into my path? Ignore her when I'm standing across from her at the church, sitting beside her during breakfast—"

"There was a hunger in your eyes."

"I was bloody famished! We didn't eat until early afternoon. Why call it a breakfast if it's not served shortly upon awakening?"

Rexton released a long-suffering sigh. "Andrew, I'm deadly serious. Gina is an innocent, and you are far too worldly for her. It is my intention to help her find a suitable husband when we return."

"Like Somerdale." He scoffed. The man had been fawning over Gina every moment she wasn't at Andrew's side. When it was her turn at the pianoforte, he'd even gone up to turn the sheets of music for her like he was a besotted swain. The display of false devotion had very nearly caused Andrew to cast up his accounts. "She won't be happy with him."

"Her happiness is not your concern."

"I disagree. She's part of the family now."

"Not. Your. Concern. Steer clear of her."

He was in need of more scotch. "As I stated earlier, she doesn't interest me in the least. And as you've stated, she is an innocent, which makes her unappealing. I suspect the girl has never even been kissed. What use would I have for her when I prefer my women to be knowledgeable in the ways of men?

Trust me, Brother, any glances or attention I bestowed upon her today was done out of politeness only. In the future, keep her away from me, so I'm not put in the position of having to be graciously attentive. It's bothersome. Especially as she is remarkably dull."

D ull, was she?

Not wanting her presence known, Gina stepped back into the shadows. She'd been sent to find her brother-in-law to let him know his wife was ready to depart. As a result she'd overheard far more of that irritating conversation than she would have liked. And to think: she'd judged Lord Andrew Mabry charming. Instead he was a boor. An oaf. Totally unsuitable for her.

Not that she'd been considering him as a possible love interest. She knew he had no wish to marry, while she had no wish to *not* marry. They'd never suit. Lord Somerdale, however, was another matter entirely. She could be happy with him. She *would* be happy with him. If he ever asked for her hand. His attentiveness seemed to come and go as frequently as she changed frocks.

She fought back the doubts stirred by Lord Andrew's words and Somerdale's failure to commit. She'd long feared that her inability to attract an assortment of beaux after her coming out had nothing to do with Tillie's scandal, but in fact was a result of her lacking in some regard. All of eleven when her mother uprooted her from New York and brought her to England so her older sister could snag herself a lord, Gina had spent a good part of the early years striving to fit in. Eventually she'd fallen in love with her adopted homeland

and became enamored of the aristocratic life. But still she was haunted by comparisons of Tillie's first Season to hers.

Tillie had been the belle of the balls, her favors sought by every bachelor in search of a wife—and even a few who weren't— her dance card always filled, flowers and chocolates delivered every day. It had been wondrous to witness, and she'd assumed she'd have the same sort of Season. Instead she'd spent the first two months of her first Season floundering, a wallflower for the most part. She tried not to take it personally but it was a bit difficult to do when one was easily hurt by the uncaring of others.

Or when one overheard conversations one shouldn't.

Hearing footsteps, she shrunk back against the shrubbery until she was certain she couldn't be seen. Holding her breath, she watched as Rexton strolled by. She was delighted the marquess intended to honor his promise to assist her in finding the proper gentleman to marry. She was equally delighted that after tonight, she would be able to limit her association with Lord Andrew. The hastily arranged preparations and all of the day's activities had kept them within close proximity. But no more. She had no wish to be in the company of a man who thought her dull.

On the other hand, perhaps she'd accept the challenge of proving him wrong.

Unnoticed, she slipped away to join her sister in the front parlor. Rexton was there, gazing on Tillie as though she were a marvel he absolutely could not get enough of.

"Ah, there you are," Gina said brightly—probably too brightly in retrospect. "I was searching for you in the library."

Not at all true, but she wasn't going to leave him with the impression she might have eavesdropped.

"I was on the terrace," he said.

"I wouldn't have thought to look there."

Tillie narrowed her eyes as though she suspected Gina of lying.

"Shouldn't you take your leave now?" Gina asked quickly, hoping to avoid an inquisition.

With a soft smile, Tillie walked over and hugged her. "Thank you for everything, dear sister."

"I didn't do anything."

"Rex and I wouldn't be together if not for you."

Pleasure warmed her face. "I'm just glad you finally moved beyond your past. I should let people know you're about to leave."

"You're to stay here while we're away," Tillie said.

With Rexton's parents, the Duke and Duchess of Greystone. "I don't really see that it's necessary I stay the entire time." Although she had brought a trunk with some of her belongings.

"You're a single woman. It wouldn't do for you to be at Landsdowne Court alone."

Gina had long resided at her sister's grand and lovely residence. "I wouldn't be alone. The servants are there."

"This is the best way to protect your reputation."

Which was crucial if she was to have any hope at all of snagging a proper gentleman.

"Besides, no one says no to my mother," Rexton said.

"It seems like a lot of bother."

"Please? So I don't worry," Tillie pleaded.

Gina rolled her eyes. "All right. I want you to enjoy your wedding trip without fretting about me."

"I'll still have some unease, just not as much. You're my little sister."

"You'll be well looked after here," Rex said.

Like a dull girl. An exciting girl would look after herself. Gina shook off the morose thoughts. She was not going to allow Lord Andrew Mabry to dwell in her mind.

Tillie hugged her again. "We'll be back next week."

Gina squeezed her tightly. "I know." They'd gone over the plans a thousand times. Seven nights at Kingsbrook Park; then she and Tillie would move into Rexton's home, while Landsdowne Court sat unused. It seemed a waste. "Don't worry about me. I'll be fine."

A few minutes later, along with all the other guests, she was tossing rose petals at Tillie and Rexton as they clambered into his waiting coach. Swallowing hard, fighting back the tears, she watched as they drove off.

People began wandering inside, but she seemed unable to move from the spot. Tillie had always been the one constant in her life.

"Here."

Glancing down, she looked at the pristine white handkerchief Lord Andrew was holding out to her. Only then did she become aware of the tears rolling along her cheeks. But she was not about to take any assistance from him. She sniffed, realizing too late how unbecoming that sounded. Nor did she want him to see her swiping at her tears.

"I don't know why women get sad at moments like this," he said quietly, gently patting his linen to her cheek, one side, then the other.

"I'm not sad. I'm happy. I'm happy that Tillie's happy." Her ability to converse intelligently seemed to have deserted her. "Aren't you happy for your brother?"

"Absolutely. His marriage takes the pressure off me to provide an heir."

She wanted to shake her head in frustration but that would cause her to move beyond reach of his tender ministrations. Only the two of them remained in the drive now. His attention was riveted on her face as though he'd only just discovered tears were wet and warm. "Aren't you pleased he's found happiness?"

"I suppose." He moved back, shrugged. "All right. Yes. I'm pleased he seems not to mind the shackles of marriage."

She heaved a sigh. "Considering your penchant for being involved with actresses, I erroneously assumed you to be a romantic."

He laughed out loud. "What do you know of my penchant?"

"I've heard things." The night she'd met him, Rexton had insinuated Andrew had been at the theater because of his interest in an actress. "In order to bring excitement to my life, I also read the gossip sheets. Otherwise, it's just so *dull*."

Taking satisfaction in his grimace, she started up the steps.

"You weren't supposed to hear that," he called after her.

"Give some thought as to how it was that I did." She glanced back over her shoulder triumphantly. "Without you even knowing I was there. I suspect, my lord, there is a good deal about me that you underestimate."

And with that parting shot, she disappeared into the residence.

CHAPTER 3

Andrew had planned to make his way to the card room and play a few hands before making a discreet exit from the affair and heading to the gaming hells. As a general rule he avoided balls. So he was quite perplexed as to the reasoning behind his now standing off to the side in the grand salon and watching as Gina was swept over the dance floor by one fellow after another.

Not that he, himself, was lacking for company. Several young ladies had approached him, fans waving, eyelashes batting, remarks teasing. He'd smiled and carried on as though he were completely engrossed by their presence, when in fact he seemed incapable of diverting his attention away from Gina.

He owed her an apology for what she'd overheard on the terrace. Most of his words had been designed to get his brother to leave off. If he'd admitted to spending a good deal of his time thinking about Gina, Rex would have hauled him off to Kingsbrook Park with him and his bride. He very nearly shuddered at that thought. His brother in love was a bit much to endure. He did wish him happiness; he just didn't think Rex needed to be quite so demonstrative with his affections.

The last lady took her feathered fan and fluttering eyelashes off in search of someone more likely to ask her to dance. He'd waltzed with a spinster, a widow, and a debutante but those forays onto the dance floor had been several tunes earlier. While he'd enjoyed his time spent with each partner, something had seemed to be missing. He probably just needed more scotch.

"You should dance with her."

He very nearly leaped out of his skin at his mother's quietly spoken words. Raised on the streets, a pickpocket in her youth, the Duchess of Greystone still had the ability to quietly sneak up on people, especially when it was one of her children up to no good.

"Lady Edith is in want of a husband," he said, referring to the woman who had just left his side. "It would not do to give her any encouragement as I'm not the marrying sort."

"I wasn't referring to her, and I think you damn well know it." His mother didn't parse words and still had a bit of the street in her. Her hair, once a vibrant red, was now muted with gray. He had little doubt he was responsible for most of it. "I meant Gina."

"Her dance card is filled." He'd managed to catch a fleeting glance at it during one of his forays onto the dance floor. Not that he'd been considering asking her for a dance. He'd simply been curious. He knew from discussions with Rex that earlier in the Season she'd had a devil of a time garnering any attention, but with her scandalous sister now married to a marquess, it seemed she was being embraced by all of London. Although his sister, Grace, Duchess of Lovingdon, might have also had a hand in that recent acceptance. She and her friends had apparently taken up Gina's cause to find a husband. Women were such a conniving lot, holding fast to the false assumption that every man was—if not in want of a wife—at least in *need* of one.

"Your father claimed her next waltz, but he's a bit tired. Perhaps you'd dance with her in his stead." Even his own mother was devious. Or perhaps it was his father. He was rather surprised the duke had asked Gina for a dance. For years his eyesight had been deteriorating. He and the duchess seldom attended balls, but when they did, the duke only danced with his duchess.

"Your older son warned me to stay clear of her."

"When have you ever heeded his orders? Besides, it's only a dance, Andrew. We want to ensure she feels welcomed into the family."

"Family obligations are so tedious."

She patted his arm affectionately. "But you'll do it."

"I suppose if I must."

"Don't sound so put upon. You don't fool me. You have an interest in the girl."

"We'd never suit."

"I once thought the same thing about your father. Yet here I am."

Chuckling, he leaned down and kissed her cheek. "I am

not proper husband material, Mother. All your machinations will not get me to the altar."

"I want merely to see you happy."

Happy seemed to be the word of the day. "I am. Very much so. I'll be even happier when I can slip away into the night, which I shall do as soon as I've taken on the obligation of Father's dance." She opened her mouth, and he gave her a stern look. "I've already stayed longer than I intended, and I have much merriment awaiting me elsewhere."

"You need a purpose, Andrew."

"I have one. To have a jolly good time." He lifted his eyebrows as the music faded. "And it appears this dance has come to an end. The next is Father's waltz. I must see to my duty."

Laughing lightly, she shook her head. "Go on and enjoy the dance, then depart to have your fun elsewhere."

"Oh, I plan to." And he left her to go in search of his dance partner.

Frannie Mabry, Duchess of Greystone, felt the hand close lovingly on her waist and the soft kiss on the nape of her neck.

"Are you sure it's wise to encourage him to have an interest in the girl?" her husband whispered near her ear, his warm breath fanning over her cheek.

"Never before have I seen him look as though he has spied something he cannot have."

"And if he hadn't been willing to take my place—after you put my name on her dance card—what then? You are well aware the only one with whom I'm comfortable dancing is you."

"We'd have worked something out," she assured him. "But I know my children. Andrew comes across as a bit of a rapscallion, but he has a good heart."

"Unfortunately I'm not quite certain it's whole, Frannie, darling."

"I fear it won't be until he opens himself up to loving again."

For a good part of the Season, Gina had lamented the scarcity of suitors and dance partners, not fully convinced Tillie's reputation was to blame. This evening, however, she'd already changed her slippers twice because she'd worn out the soles. Every dance had been claimed. She was looking quite forward to the next one—her waltz with the Duke of Greystone. Knowing of his failing eyesight, which few did, she was rather certain she'd be able to convince him to sit this one out or at the very least step out onto the terrace for a bit of fresh air.

Although standing at the edge of the dance floor, searching for him, she was beginning to wonder if perhaps he'd forgotten about the dance he'd claimed—or rather that his wife had claimed for him. She was fairly certain signing the small dance card would no doubt have been a challenge for him.

When she saw Andrew striding in her direction, she couldn't seem to stop herself from stiffening. Silly girl. No reason to believe he was actually going to approach her. His next dance partner was no doubt in the vicinity. She fought not to care or to wonder who she might be. His partners thus far had surprised her as two had been older and the third was on the verge of receiving a marriage proposal if rumors were to be believed. Not the sorts in whom she'd expect him to take an interest. The flamboyant seemed more his style.

While he smiled and nodded at several ladies, his gloved hands remained at his side, did not reach out for a partner. Perhaps he was merely heading for the terrace, although there was a more direct path.

Her stomach tightened as she realized his gaze was homed in on her. His blue eyes seemed to glow with amusement as he came to a stop in front of her and held out his hand.

"My father has grown weary. Perhaps you'd be willing to allow me to dance in his stead."

No, no, no. They'd danced once before—at the ball where Rexton proposed to Tillie—so she was well aware that being held by Lord Andrew caused strange flutterings to take up residence throughout her body. *Yes, yes, yes.* Because those flutterings were quite pleasant indeed.

Based upon what she'd overheard earlier on the terrace, she should rebuff him and his overtures. Before she could work out the exact words for the caustic remark that would put him in his place, she heard herself say, "If that would please the duke."

With an arched brow, he glanced down at his extended hand. Reluctantly she placed hers in it, trying to ignore the warmth seeping through the kidskin as he closed his fingers around hers. The first strains of the tune began to fill the air as he led her to the center of the dance floor.

When his hand landed gently on her back, she was at once grateful for the low cut of her gown and wishing it went all the way up to her hairline. As she placed her hand on his arm, near his shoulder, she was as astounded by the firmness of his muscles as she'd been the first time they'd danced. While he was lean, he was strong and fit. Placing her other hand in his, she tried to ignore how very close they were. And the fact he was quite possibly the most graceful partner she'd ever had.

"I noticed you danced twice with Somerdale," he said.

"I've danced with a lot of gents."

"Not twice."

She took some satisfaction in knowing he was not only watching but counting. Especially as, to her mortification, she'd been doing the same thing with him. "I would dance with him more often than that, but dancing with a gentleman more than twice is scandalous. Having survived Tillie's scandal, I have no wish to deal with one of my own, so alas I must limit my dances per gentleman to two. However, I am flattered you noticed."

"Do you fancy him?" he asked.

"I don't really see that's any of your concern."

"He's a spendthrift."

"And you're not?"

"I don't lose at the gaming tables."

"Well, that's certainly a trait every woman highly covets in a man."

"It should be if it's your money with which he's gambling."

"Your brother is advising me. I don't need you to do it as well."

"My brother doesn't move about in the same . . . *questionable* circles that I do."

"Yet Somerdale does?"

"On occasion."

"Why do you care?" she asked, not bothering to hide her irritation.

"You're part of the family now. I don't want to see you hurt."

"I appreciate your concern, but I'm fully capable of taking care of myself. Any gentleman who seeks to make a fool of me will find himself regretting it."

He grinned broadly. "Oh. And how will you accomplish that? By writing a stern letter to the *Times*, calling him out?"

"By shooting him someplace he'd rather not be shot."

He laughed. "With a pistol?"

"Or a rifle. My family is in the firearms business. Surely you're not surprised to discover I'm proficient in using both."

"Perhaps I am a little. I'd never really given it any thought." His eyes warmed. "What other things don't I know about you, Miss Hammersley?"

The pressure on her back was subtle, yet she was very much aware of the fact that they were a little closer. She should have objected, but she welcomed the nearness. From the moment she'd been introduced to him at the theater, he'd intrigued her. "First, tell me something I don't know about you."

"That I can see the thrumming of your pulse at your throat and would very much like to feel it against my tongue."

CHAPTER 4

Christ. Had he really just said that? Rex was correct. Andrew needed to stay not only away from her, but far, far away from her. She was too innocent for the likes of him, and whenever he was near her, he seemed to misplace all rational thought.

Those beautiful green eyes of hers widened and her pale pink lips parted slightly, but the distance between them was narrow enough that if he lowered his head, he could press his mouth to hers and slip his tongue inside without meeting any resistance. Unless, of course, she was carrying a pistol upon her person. He very nearly asked.

"You're attempting to shock me," she said tersely.

Dear God, how he wished that was all it was. Instead he wanted to lift her into his arms and carry her up to his old bedchamber, lay her out on his bed, and ravage her until dawn. He wanted to know the taste of her, every inch. Her mouth, her throat, her breasts, the sweet haven between her thighs. He yearned to sip them all at his leisure, to take her slowly and wickedly, to hear her sighs and moans filling his ears. He'd told Rex he found her dull when in truth she was the furthest thing from dull he'd ever known.

"Does Somerdale not make such claims?" he asked lightly.

"Of course not. He is a gentleman."

"A boring one at that, then."

"You know, my lord, if I didn't know better I'd almost think you were jealous."

He scoffed, a bit too loudly, as the couple nearby glanced over at him. "I've never been jealous in my life. That particular emotion is reserved for those who seek permanence in a relationship."

"You've never been in love?"

The question caused his stomach to tighten, the sadness in her eyes made him want to lash out. He fought back the urge by making his voice as frigid as possible. "Have you?"

She shook her head. "No, which to be quite honest I find a bit disheartening. At the ripe old age of nineteen, it seems that at least once I should have fallen in love, possibly had my heart broken."

"A broken heart serves no use. Trust me on that."

"Have you had your heart broken?"

Not in any manner to which he was willing to admit. "I have heard musings on the subject of broken hearts from those who have."

She studied him as though she suspected him of attempting to divert the discussion from his own past. After all these years, he still couldn't admit the truth regarding the naivete he'd shown in his youth. The music ended. Thank

God. They'd begun traveling down a path he did not wish to follow, one that would lead to the resurrection of memories best left buried. Holding her gaze, he brought her gloved hand to his lips, pressed a kiss to her fingers. "You will find love, Miss Hammersley. I've no doubt of that."

"How can you be so sure?"

"Gentlemen prefer heiresses. You shall have a slew of beaux from whom to choose. Don't settle on Somerdale until you've seen the other offerings."

"Do you prefer heiresses?"

One in particular but she was far too dangerous, too alluring. "Only the ones who are already married."

"Why are you so opposed to marriage?" she asked, disappointment registering in her eyes. He kept his face a mask so as not to reveal that he detested disappointing her.

"The same woman every night for the remainder of my life? Why give up the feast for porridge every day?"

"You have a cynical view that does you no good. Even porridge needn't always be served the same way. I find your thinking lacks imagination if you don't see that."

"Trust me, Miss Hammersley, my imagination isn't at fault here." But damned if she didn't make a good point. He suspected every day with her would be filled with surprises.

A clearing of a throat had him glancing over at Lord Manville.

"I believe the next dance is mine?" the viscount asked hesitantly as though he wasn't quite certain Andrew would give up his claim on the lady.

What could she possibly see in the gap-toothed man? Still

Andrew was not going to become jealous of a gent who barely reached his shoulder. He bowed slightly, only then realizing he had yet to release his hold on her hand. "Of course." He turned his attention back to her. "Thank you, Miss Hammersley. It was an enlightening conversation."

Striding away, he couldn't help but wonder exactly how she liked her *porridge* served.

Sitting in his father's library, sipping on scotch, Andrew cursed the strange fascination he had with Gina. He'd ended up staying until the last guest left, remaining in the ballroom and tormenting himself by watching her dance, flirt, and laugh with an assortment of gentlemen, all unsuitable for her. Considering her diminutive height, some were too tall—including himself if he were honest. Some too short. Others too plump or too thin or odd looking. She'd even danced with Lord Wheatley, whose face was a permanent mottled red that made him look as though he walked around in a constant state of embarrassment. Did she really want a child who resembled that unfortunate fellow? Like begat like. Perhaps he should hand her a book on husbandry and explain how breeding worked.

Gina and his parents had retired for the night. His mother had suggested he stay, rather than heading to his townhouse, but how could he when he knew *she* was sleeping down the hallway, only a few doors from his room? He imagined if he listened very carefully he would be able to hear her breathing in slumber.

As much as he fought it, he envisioned more than her breathing. He saw himself standing beside her bed, gazing down on her as she slept, unmoving until finally, at last, she opened her eyes, smiled softly, and lifted the covers in invitation.

All he imagined was the sight of bared shoulders, yet he grew so hard he ached. What the devil was wrong with him? Obviously he'd been too long without a woman. It had been weeks since he'd parted ways with the actress, and he'd not sought out a replacement—not even for a single night. That was the reason for his mind's lustful wanderings when it came to Gina.

Well, he knew the cure and just where to find it.

Gazing out the window, Gina had yet to see Andrew leave. Although he could have made his exit while she was changing out of her gown and into her nightdress. As she'd started up the stairs, she'd overheard the duchess imploring him to stay the night. Perhaps at this very moment he was stretched out on a bed, staring at the canopy, and thinking of her.

She scoffed at that fantasy. He considered her dull. Although he'd admitted to wanting to lay his tongue against her pulse. At the thought, warmth sluiced through her just as it had when he'd spoken the words in a raspy voice as though the mere idea of it dried his throat. It had certainly dried hers.

It was long past midnight. She should be abed, but how could she sleep when memories of the day bombarded her, all the moments when she'd been in his company? She'd engaged in conversation with other gentlemen, danced with them, but the memory of the time spent with them was rapidly fading like fog withering before the sun. While every recollection of Andrew seemed only to brighten in intensity.

Slumber would elude her. Perhaps a book would help. While she was only a guest, she was familiar with the residence, having spent considerable time here after Tillie became betrothed. She was certain the duke wouldn't mind her prowling about his library. Perhaps she'd even nip a bit of brandy. That should help her sleep.

After slipping into her wrap, she headed into the hallway and down the stairs. In the foyer, she turned into the hallway. The residence was still and quiet. Everyone lost to dreams except for her. Brandy was definitely called for—after finding a book. Entering the library, she found her nose very nearly flattened against a broad chest.

"You're still here," she said to Andrew, hating that she sounded breathless, excited, and grateful all at once.

"Looking for me?"

Yes. No. "I was in search of a book to read. I couldn't sleep, but then I seldom can after a ball. All the excitement of the evening is still whirring through my brain. Perhaps you'd be up for some cribbage."

He made a face as though she'd suggested needlepoint. "I'm on my way out."

"Home or elsewhere?"

"Elsewhere."

"As I'm unable to sleep, I'll go with you then, shall I?"

He gave her a patronizing grin. "It's not the sort of place ladies usually visit."

"Is it one of those questionable places you mentioned earlier? I know you think me dull, but I'm actually quite adventurous. Do you know when Tillie would go out at night to be with Rexton, I'd often sneak off to the Twin Dragons." The establishment was a private club offering wagering, spirits, and dancing that catered to men and women.

"This place is nothing at all like the Twin Dragons."

"Then I'm even more keen to go. I enjoy partaking in new experiences."

His gaze wandered slowly over her as though he were marking every line, dip, and curve. "You're not dressed for going out."

"I can be. Give me half an hour."

"I've yet to meet a woman who can get properly dressed in half an hour."

"I can. Give me a chance. When Tillie returns I'll have no freedom whatsoever."

The sensual curling up of his lips stole her breath. His expression told her they were on the verge of doing something truly wicked. "Be quick about it."

She released a tiny squeal and hopped before making a mad dash into the hallway.

"Grab a wrap with a hood," he called after her. "We'll need to be sure you're not recognized."

CHAPTER 5

"Is this a brothel?"

She didn't sound scandalized, merely curious. He didn't know what had prompted him to bring her here. Granted, it was where he'd planned to come before she showed up in the library begging to go with him on his adventure. He did wish he hadn't insisted she keep the hood of her pelisse raised. It shaded her face from him, and he desperately wanted to see the blush he was certain was presently warming her cheeks.

"Ah, you are a mistress of deduction. What gave it away?" he asked.

She snapped her head around, lifted her face to his in order to hold his gaze, causing the hood to fall back just enough that the dim lighting allowed him to see the curiosity in her eyes. "They're not wearing frocks. Only corsets and skirts which show a good deal of ankle."

"Saves time. I suppose you can wait in the parlor while I—"

"*Mon chère*, it's been a while." The voice was throaty, the accent French.

He turned to the buxom woman with hair a red shade he doubted nature had ever created. She was no longer in the blossom of youth, her face reflecting a life that had known a good deal of hardship. Still, he took her hand, pressed a kiss to the pudgy fingers. "Madame Elise. I fear I have neglected your establishment for far too long."

She tossed her head Gina's way. "Who is your lovely companion?"

"Let's simply refer to her as Miss H."

"So you want something a little different tonight. Is it to be one girl for the two of you to share or one for each of you?"

"One for each of us," Gina said, stepping forward.

Andrew stared at her. Had she gone mad? When he had insinuated he was going to get on with business while she waited, she was supposed to return to the carriage in a huff or at the very least announce he was to take her home. He'd brought her here to teach her a lesson: adventures could carry consequences, especially when she didn't know where the adventures might lead.

Madame Elise smiled with the sort of sauciness he suspected accompanied her often during her youth. "Oh, I like your spirit, *mademoiselle*."

Clearing his throat he leaned down and lowered his voice. "I don't think you quite understand what she is implying."

"Oh, I understand perfectly." Gina pointed discreetly. "The girl with the black hair and the red corset. I rather like the looks of her. I do get to choose, don't I?"

He was on the verge of blurting, "No!" when the madam said, "Of course, *ma chère*." She snapped her fingers at the brunette, who immediately shot off the sofa where she'd been lounging.

"I'm not certain this is a good idea," Andrew said, taking pride in the fact he managed to sound calm. He'd expected Gina to retreat, not rush forward into the fray. Rex was going to kill him if he ever learned about this outing.

"Oh, I think it's a splendid idea. You won't believe how often I've considered doing this, but I didn't know where to go or how to manage the particulars. I'm frightfully excited about all the possibilities."

His head nearly exploded as a variety of sexual positions burst through his mind. "You are aware that we are talking about sex occurring here."

"Of course. I'm not a dimwit. I understand the purpose of brothels. Although I haven't any coins. Would you be so kind as to pay for tonight's adventure? I can reimburse you on the morrow."

Before he could say no, the madam once again interfered. "Your first time, *ma chére*, is on the house."

The dark-haired beauty sidled up to Gina, dipped a little, and slid up her body, very much like a cat. His mouth went dry, his cock twitched. Damn it to hell.

Smiling brightly, Gina looked over at him. "See you in a bit."

The girl took Gina's hand and began leading her toward the stairs.

"Now we need to find someone for you, *mon cher*," Madame Elise said.

"Yes, I am in need of a woman," he announced loudly. "A buxom one at that."

Gina didn't even look back.

"With wide hips!"

She started up the stairs. He watched until she reached the landing, disappeared down a hallway. He waited on bated breath, expecting her to pop back out and laugh, flinging her arms wide and proclaiming, "I was only teasing."

Only she didn't reappear, no matter how hard he wished it.

"She's a saucy one. Wherever did you find 'er?" Elise asked, her cockney suddenly strong. Apparently she'd forgotten she was supposed to be French, although any self-respecting Frenchman would be offended by her accent.

He glared at her, wanting to blame her for this fiasco but knowing the fault rested with him for being foolish enough not to stand firm against Gina's imploring green eyes. "Have you ever had a woman customer?"

"We 'ave all sorts, love."

"How long does it take?"

She glanced up the stairs, rolled a shoulder carelessly. "I'd give 'em an hour. Now who would ye like to entertain ye while yer waiting?"

He let scotch entertain him. It wasn't the best he'd ever had, but it dulled the senses as he stood with his back against the wall, his gaze fastened on the top of the stairs. He tried not to envision what was happening in that room—

Bloody hell. He couldn't seem to stop the images from flashing through his mind, because he knew exactly what was taking place. When he was nineteen, younger and curious, he'd paid to watch two girls pleasuring each other. In all fairness, he'd hoped to learn a few techniques he could incorporate into his own lovemaking arsenal. He'd wanted to bring his lover at the time as much pleasure as a man could bring a woman. He'd been open to trying anything. So he'd watched and learned and embarrassed himself because his young randy self had never seen anything so sensual. There had been no rush to fruition. There had been nothing left untouched, unkissed, unlicked.

So he knew precisely what was happening. Gina's clothes were slowly being removed. Bared skin would be kissed. Breasts would be suckled. Hands would caress—

He dug out his watch. Only a quarter of an hour had passed. Three more. Three more quarters of an hour to endure. He would go mad with—

He hesitated to use the word jealousy. He was not the jealous sort. Yet what he was experiencing now made him feel as though his skin were too tight, that his entire being was on the verge of combusting.

Visions of Gina being touched in ways that he wanted to touch her, stroke her, caress her bombarded him. It didn't matter that she was with a woman. He'd have felt the same if she was with a man. It was the act itself, the things being done to her, the way she would squirm, thrash about, cry out in ecstasy.

What if she hadn't understood precisely what was going to happen in that room? What if she didn't know how to extricate herself from an uncomfortable situation? What if she thought she had to go through with something even if she didn't want it? She could be in need of rescuing and he'd never know. What the deuce had he been thinking to let her go off with the girl? He'd been irresponsible, could not risk that she might be in trouble with no way of calling out to him.

He shoved himself away from the wall and stormed across the room to where Elise was sprawled in a chair. "Which room?"

"Once a client has gone upstairs, we don't disturb them." Her French accent had returned.

To hell with that. If he had to search every room, he was going to bloody well disturb them until his mind was put at ease. "Which room?"

"If you partake, I will charge you. If you watch—"

He dug some coins out of his pocket and tossed them at her. "Name your price. I'll send more over tomorrow."

She gave him a victorious grin, as though she knew he was being spurred by jealousy. He was not, he absolutely was not. It was concern for Gina, pure and simple.

"The purple door."

He charged up the stairs and down the hallway in which Gina had disappeared. While he hadn't been here in years, he knew the doors had no locks. If a girl screamed, they wanted to be able to get to her easily. And the knowledge that the doors could be opened stopped some gents from being rougher than they might be otherwise.

As he rushed toward the purple door, he decided he'd just throw it open, calmly instruct Gina to get dressed, and close the door. It would have more impact without a knock to forewarn them and perhaps she'd listen. If he yelled at her through the door, she was likely to carry on. Besides, he didn't want to disturb the other customers, have them dashing out into the hallway to see what all the fuss was about. He was striving for discretion in order to protect her reputation.

He barged in and staggered to a stop. They were sitting on the bed, legs crossed, knees nearly touching as they leaned toward each other, possibly on their way to engaging in a kiss. "We're leaving," he announced without preamble.

"But I'm not finished here."

That was obvious. She was still fully clothed, as was the girl. Not a single stitch had yet to be removed, not a hair out of place. Thank God, he'd arrived before any mischief or real damage could occur. "Well, I am. Let's go."

She looked at the girl. "So he's a quick bugger?"

"A what?" he snapped.

"Not usually," the girl said. "At least that's what I hear. I've never had the pleasure of his lordship's company."

"What the devil are you on about?" he asked, irritated to be the subject of their conversation, to have them discussing him as though he wasn't even in the room.

Gina glanced over at him, her face a mask of innocence. "Venus—"

"Venus? Good God, are you serious?" She'd named herself after the goddess of love?

"Don't interrupt. Anyway, she was explaining that some men are rather quick at peaking, which a prostitute doesn't mind because then she can go on to her next john. That's what they call you, you know? It doesn't matter what your real name is. To them you're just john. But a woman who isn't being paid—like a wife for example—wants a gent who isn't quick. She wants a man with stamina, who can go on for a while because it takes women a bit longer to peak. And if a man is always fast, a woman might never experience absolute pleasure. Why do you suppose nature did it that way?"

What was she going on about? "Which way?"

"Made it more of a challenge for women to reach orgasm. That's what it's called. Orgasm. My vocabulary has expanded dramatically since sitting here talking with Venus."

"That's what you've been doing? Sitting there talking?"

"Yes, but back to the orgasm question. It doesn't seem fair."

God help him, he burst out laughing.

"What's so funny?" she asked.

"Of all the things I'd imagined going on in here, talking was not one of them."

"What did you imagine?"

He abruptly sobered and cleared his throat. "We should be off."

"But I have so much more to learn."

"I know a better way to teach you. Come on."

She scrambled off the bed. When she reached him, she placed her hand on his arm and while it was as light as a butterfly landing on a petal, he felt it as though he wore no jacket, no shirt. "You'll still pay her, won't you? Even though we only talked, even though Madame Elise said there would be no charge. It's not fair to Venus not to make any money after giving me her time."

"I'll see that she's paid double." *Because they'd only talked.*

The look of gratitude she bestowed upon him caused a funny, unfamiliar sensation—a tightening that wasn't altogether unpleasant—in his chest.

She started to walk past him.

"Cover yourself with the hood." While he'd waited in the parlor he'd spotted a couple of gents—one who had danced with her earlier in the evening—escort girls up the stairs. The last thing he needed was to have one of them exiting a room and spying her in the hallway.

When they were clear of the room, he was grateful when she took his arm and snuggled up against him as though she saw him as her protector. Although he was so far removed from being that he'd probably burn in hell. "You do realize you are never to tell anyone I brought you here," he said, his voice low.

"It'll be our secret," she whispered back, and he wished he wasn't bombarded with other words he'd like to have her murmur to him.

He led her down another hallway, this one narrow and short. A behemoth of a man stood guard outside a door. Andrew handed him a coin. The bloke nodded once before opening the door for them.

Andrew escorted Gina inside. When the door closed, they were engulfed in darkness save for a single pinprick of light. The rule for this room was that it was for private viewing so he knew they wouldn't be disturbed.

"We must be very quiet," he told her, his voice merely a whisper of sound. His eyes had adjusted to the darkness so he was able to see her silhouette nod. He guided her toward the peephole. "Look through there."

Leaning in, she peered into the next room. With a gasp, she jumped back, her elbow jabbing him in the ribs. He bit back his grunt.

"There is a man and woman in there," she whispered harshly, quickly, the words running together. "Nude."

She sounded absolutely horrified. "What were they doing?"

"Sitting on a bed."

"You said you wanted to be educated."

"You're not implying I watch them."

"I am."

"That's unconscionable. To spy on people—"

"They want you to." He shrugged. "Well, at least he does. That's what he's paying for. The gent to whom I gave a coin is going to knock on their door and let them know they have an audience. That's what they've been waiting for."

"Why would they want that?"

"He enjoys being watched, is thrilled by the notion of performing. They don't mind if you look."

"Have you watched couples?"

"When I was much, much younger, curious, and determined not to make a fool of myself during my first encounter."

He heard her swallow. "You're certain they don't mind?"

"Absolutely certain."

She eased back to the wall, leaned in. He moved nearer, lowered himself until his mouth was near her ear, near that pulse that so intrigued him.

"What are they doing?" he asked.

"Do you want to look?"

"No, I want you to tell me."

She swallowed again. "They're standing there, kissing. Not their mouths but each other's throat and shoulders."

He was tempted to do the same, to press his lips to the nape of her neck but if he did, he'd be lost. So he tormented himself by merely inhaling her fragrance, allowing the scent of violets to inhabit his nostrils and lungs, intoxicating him in ways he'd never before experienced.

"Do you look like that?" she asked.

"Like what precisely?"

"Do you have that belly?"

"I'll have to take a peek."

She moved only her head aside. He peered through the hole. The room was shadowy but the low flame in the lamp cast a golden glow over the couple. The gent was an older man, not someone he knew. He carried something of a paunch about with him. He backed away, allowing her access to the viewing room, returning his lips to the vicinity of her ear. "No." He drew the word out, long and low.

"His . . . member."

"Surely Venus taught you a better word than that for it," he teased.

"I can't quite bring myself to say it. Are they all like that?"

He almost insisted she repeat what she'd been taught, but he didn't want to force anything on her. He wanted her to say it of her own accord. It would be so much sexier then— although the last thing he needed was her sexier. In the darkness with her scent, her warmth, her raspy voice, he was struggling to rein in his desires. "Some are longer, thicker."

"Do you speak from experience?"

"Perhaps. What is she doing now?"

"Going down to her knees." She spun around, her chin slamming against his nose. *Christ, that hurt.* "I don't think I want to see the actual act."

"Why ever not?"

"It's such a private thing. It's seems wrong to watch, even if it's what they want. I'll trust my husband to show me how to do it properly."

"There is no properly. It's like porridge. As I was recently reminded, it can be served in many different ways."

"Are you a connoisseur, then?"

"I know a few things." If she were the sort with whom he could use actions rather than words, he might have shared his knowledge. Instead he decided it was time to put an end to this adventure before he succumbed to the temptation of her and did something that would irrevocably change the course of their lives. "It's late. I should return you to the residence."

As the carriage traveled through London, Gina stared out the window into the darkness. She should be tired. Instead she was more invigorated. Unable to stop thinking about the woman going to her knees, she wondered what she might have been planning to do from that position. Perhaps she should have watched. She was rather disappointed in herself for not being as daring as she'd always believed herself to be. "Do you think me a coward?"

"Why would I think that?" He sat across from her, his legs stretched out, his booted feet resting on either side of hers.

"Because you presented me with an opportunity to learn

something I stated I wanted to learn, and then when confronted with it, I wavered . . . and retreated."

"I think it took more courage to turn away knowing I was likely never to let you forget you had."

"You do realize it took a measure of trust in you for me to stay. I hope I don't come to discover it was misplaced."

"It wasn't. It'll always be our secret." They weren't traveling with a lantern burning so it was difficult to see him but she could make out his silhouette as he leaned forward, and she imagined his elbows pressing into his thighs. "Gina, you should never worry about being perceived as a coward if you're not comfortable with something, especially when it comes to intimate moments with a man. Whether it is a gent who is courting you or one who has wed you—if he is asking or demanding something of you that you'd rather not do, tell him in no uncertain terms to bugger off."

His phrasing made her smile, his advice warmed her. "Women are expected to obey their husbands."

"Ah, but you have an advantage. You have the ability to shoot him, in a spot where he'd rather not be shot."

Laughing at the absurd notion she truly would threaten her husband with a pistol, she thought things would be so much simpler if she didn't like him so much. "Was that house of ill repute really your original destination when we crossed paths in the library? Or did you alter your plans in an attempt to shock me?"

He leaned back, taking his bergamot and lemony fragrance with him. "I kept to my plans . . . thinking they would shock you. As things turned out, I was the one surprised."

She'd surprised herself. "I couldn't pass up the opportunity to speak with a woman of experience about what transpires between a man and woman. Tillie and I have never spoken of the details. Like you, I don't want to make a fool of myself the first time."

"You could have asked me."

"That would have been highly inappropriate."

"Yet going to a brothel with me wasn't?"

Her face warmed. She didn't think she could have gone with anyone else. She'd spoken true. She did trust him. And not only because he was Rex's brother, but because she sensed he would protect her at all costs. And he'd always shown her kindness. While his attention had seemed brotherly on the surface, she'd often felt an undercurrent of desire simmering through him. Or perhaps it was only wishful thinking on her part. He'd never done anything untoward. *More's the pity.* "I didn't know that's where we were going until we got there."

"Lesson learned. Never traipse off with a gent until you know exactly where he is taking you and precisely what his intentions are."

"So tonight was a lesson for me, was it?"

"You seemed to make it so. What did she teach you?"

She was grateful for the darkness because she was relatively certain her face was sporting a mottled blush. "They were not things to be discussed with a man."

"Yet they are things to be done with a man."

More, it was things to *know* about a man. "I'm not going to divulge the details of what I might have learned. It is for me to know."

"And for me to find out?"

Heat swamped her as she envisioned how he might find out, with her showing him. Venus had explained how a man's body worked and all the places where he was most sensitive, how to touch him with her hands and her mouth. She squeezed her eyes shut, realizing at last why the girl had gone down on her knees.

"Share with me some of the vocabulary words she taught you."

Her eyes sprung open. "I'm certain you know them all."

"Perhaps I don't. Tonight might turn out to be a lesson for me as well."

"Perhaps you will have learned I'm not so dull after all."

His harsh curse rent through the confines of the carriage, and she regretted that she'd ruined his jovial mood.

"Gina, I don't find you dull."

"You said you did." She hated that her voice sounded as though it was surrounded by tears. He'd spoken with her at the theater. He'd instructed her on how to increase her odds of winning at the roulette table one night when they'd crossed paths at the Twin Dragons. He'd waltzed with her at the ball where Rex had proposed. When Tillie had accepted, Andrew had leaned down and whispered, "Well that will change things between us."

She hadn't known precisely what he meant. She supposed that they would be related in some distant way.

"I was striving to get Rex to leave off," he said now. "He was warning me to stay away from you, not for the first time. I didn't need the lecture. I am well aware your reputation must take precedence above all else if you are to secure a good marriage. I want that for you. I'm not going to do something untoward that puts your future happiness at risk."

"Tonight seemed rather untoward."

"Things that take place within the shadows of the night need never see the light of day. No one will find out about our little excursion. Besides, you initiated it." He sighed. "Although I shouldn't have accepted the temptation."

"Do you find me tempting?"

"I was referring to the temptation of teasing you. I view you as a sister."

That was disappointing. "So you would have taken Grace there?"

"Absolutely not. My sister doesn't need to know about the things going on in a place like that."

She laughed. "She's married! She is *doing* the things that occur in a place like that."

"Good God! Don't make me start thinking about what Lovingdon might be doing with her. I'm rather certain she's still a virgin."

"She has children."

"Who came about through immaculate conception. And you do realize this conversation is inappropriate."

"The entire night has been inappropriate."

"So it has been."

But she heard a smile in his voice. "I rather enjoyed it. Thank you for allowing me to tag along."

"I'll never be able to go back there now without seeing you

traipsing up the stairs with a harlot. You may have bloody well ruined it for me."

A part of her was glad. She didn't like thinking of him with other women. "Do you go there often?"

"Not in years."

"You prefer actresses."

"I prefer women who are a bit more discerning with their favors."

"What was she like tonight, the woman you were with?"

"An unexpected delight."

"You should have spent a bit more time with her then."

"I was in her company for most of the night."

His words took her aback, forcefully, as though she'd been punched. "I was asking after the woman you bedded."

"Surely Venus taught you another word for that."

"It's too harsh sounding. I don't like it. So I won't use it. And you're avoiding the question."

"I wasn't with anyone else tonight, Gina," he said quietly.

She wondered how long it would be before her lungs began to work again and take in air.

He looked out the window. "Almost there."

The carriage slowed, turned onto the drive. The adventure was coming to a close. She rather wished it wasn't. But at least she was breathing again.

They stopped. Andrew immediately opened the door, leaped out, then reached back for her, extending his hand. It was ungloved. She supposed he'd taken them off as they'd journeyed home. She placed her gloved palm on his bare skin. He assisted her out of the conveyance. Rather than releasing his hold on her, he tucked her hand within the crook of his elbow and escorted her up the walk, up the steps, stopping at the door.

"I don't find you dull, Gina."

Facing him, she looked up at him. He was so much taller than she, yet she wouldn't mind gazing up at him forever, even if it made her neck ache.

"You have intrigued me from the moment I met you," he continued.

"Yet you avoid me."

Holding her gaze, he skimmed his warm fingers along her cheek. "You are the sort men marry." He leaned down. She cursed the faint light from the gaslights that kept her from seeing the blue of his eyes. "I am not the marrying sort."

"Why?"

"Because I have no heart. You deserve a man with not only a heart, but a title. You deserve so much that I cannot give you."

He was so close now. She waited, waited for him to traverse that final inch. She felt her pulse throbbing. *Lay your tongue against it, calm it, then press your mouth to mine.* She licked her lips. There was an audible hitch in his breath. He came half an inch closer.

Yes, be the first to ever kiss me. Show me what desire feels like.

Abruptly he straightened, inserted a key into the lock, swung the door open, and peered inside. "All clear. In with you."

His voice sounded raspy and raw as though he'd gone weeks without water. She wanted to protest, but she feared if she asked for a kiss, he'd rebuff her. They'd have years of seeing each other at family gatherings. She wanted nothing to create awkwardness between them. Taking a deep breath, she stepped over the threshold and into the foyer.

"Sleep well, Gina."

She spun around. "You're not staying the night?"

He shook his head.

"I suppose you're headed back to the brothel." She hated the thought of him going there.

"No, I'm rather worn out. I'll be seeking the comfort of my own bed."

It was irritating that so much relief washed through her. "Sweet dreams, then."

He winked. "I'd rather have wicked ones."

Leaving her there, he drew the door to a close behind him. She heard the key going into the lock, him jogging down the steps, the clatter of the carriage as it departed.

Turning on her heel she headed for the stairs with a wry grin. Considering all Venus had explained to her in the short time they were together, she was rather certain that her own slumber was going to be filled with wicked fantasies as well.

Unfortunately, she feared they might all involve him.

He'd almost kissed her.

Stretched out on the seat in his carriage, he couldn't deny that fact. Standing there on the steps within an inch of her luscious mouth, with her scent wafting around him, he'd almost leaned in and closed the gap between them. What a mistake that would have been, because he already recognized that, with her, one kiss wouldn't have been enough. He'd have wanted more: a hundred, a thousand.

Of further alarm was the fact that he was fairly certain he'd have not been able to stop with only a kiss. He wanted to touch her in ways he'd envisioned Venus touching her. He wanted her sighs ringing in his ears, her moans tightening his muscles. He wanted the silkiness of her skin captured within his palm.

He couldn't remember the last time he'd enjoyed a night so much or been so enthralled by the company of a woman. Her little triumphant smiles when she thought she'd gotten the better of him warmed him to his core.

The night he met her, he'd been involved with an actress and had gone to the theater in order to watch her performance. He'd stepped into Rex's theater box, expecting it to be empty. Instead he'd found Rex there with two ladies: the notorious Lady Landsdowne and her far too innocent sister. He preferred women with experience, yet Gina had beguiled him.

Soon after, he'd ended things with the actress, and he hadn't been with a woman since. He wouldn't go to one now, not after being in Gina's company for most of the night.

Yet in order to retain his sanity and ensure he did nothing to compromise her chances of finding a respectable match, he needed to avoid her as though she carried the plague. No more adventures, no more dares, no more nights of utter contentment and secretive smiles. No more temptation.

He would bury himself in play and strive to forget how badly he wanted her.

CHAPTER 6

It was shortly after noon before Gina awoke. Fortunately, she was able to blame all the wedding activities and festivities for her sluggish start to the day when the duchess asked after her with concern. Although in truth it was her adventures during the wee hours that were responsible. Not that she was going to admit that to anyone other than herself.

But she couldn't seem to stop thinking about it as she visited in the parlor with one gentleman caller after another while the duchess kindly sat in a corner with her writing desk in her lap, scribbling away, serving as chaperone.

Her fifth caller, Lord Somerdale, was presently sipping tea with her. Flowers from half a dozen men had been delivered throughout the day. Word had either spread that she was residing in the Greystone residence until Tillie returned from her wedding trip or the servants at Landsdowne Court were directing the deliveries and gents here. She suspected it was a little bit of both. Nothing happened in London without everyone knowing. Well, except for forays to brothels in the dead of night.

"That's a rather mysterious smile," Somerdale said, arching a brow in curiosity. "What are you thinking?"

"My apologies, my lord. My mind drifted off to yesterday and how happy Tillie appeared to be." Oh dear. Lies came so easily today. Was that a result of Andrew's influence? "You were saying?"

"You deserve to be as happy."

"You were saying that?"

He blushed. "Well, no, I was waxing on about Byron's writings. I know you're fond of reading."

"And walks in the park. What say we step out for a while? To be quite honest, I've had about all the tea I can stand today."

He perked up. "I'd like that very much."

She glanced over at her hostess. "Would that meet with your approval, Duchess? If we go for a short stroll? My maid can serve as chaperone." To ensure her presence wouldn't be too much of a burden on the Greystone staff, she'd brought Annie with her.

"I think it's a lovely day for an outing. Go with my blessing."

Sometime later she and Somerdale were strolling arm in arm through Hyde Park. Every now and then a gentleman would walk or ride by—in a carriage or on a horse—and tip his hat to her. Amazing the attention one garnered when no longer associated with scandal. She found it somewhat of a relief to have some confirmation that her uneventful Season had not rested squarely upon her shoulders.

"I've not seen you at the Twin Dragons of late," Somerdale said.

"I've been frightfully busy. The wedding came about in such a rush."

He chuckled. "I daresay you have the right of that. There are wagers at White's on Rexton's heir arriving within eight months."

"Truly." She didn't bother to hide her irritation that men would wager on something that was none of their business, or that they still considered Tillie scandalous enough to find herself with child before she was married—although Gina knew there was a chance she could be with child. But if she was, her sister would have told her, would have gone ahead and shared the joy. Tillie had long wanted a child, but she'd been unlucky in that regard during her first marriage. "What position did you take on the wager?"

His cheeks reddening, he cleared his throat, looked down at the grass as though the answer resided there. "I wagered it would come early . . . in seven months."

"Pity. You'll not be collecting on that wager."

His look was one of incredulity. "She's not with child?"

"No. Did no one consider they married in haste because they wanted to be together so desperately? They're frightfully in love. I found the whole affair terribly romantic."

"I've offended you."

"Disappointed more like. I want someone to love me to distraction just as Rexton loves her, to insist the wedding take place immediately so we might be together."

"Marry in haste, repent in leisure. One should not rush into these things."

"Marry in leisure and you might have the woman doubting your devotion to her."

"You're quite right. Marrying in haste is the way to go. What are your thoughts on courtship? Should it go just as quickly?"

"I suppose it depends on the couple and their relationship, as well as what they feel for each other."

"I adore you."

She stopped and stared at him. His blunt admission was unexpected. She'd been rather certain he fancied her, but he'd given no previous hint his affections ran so deeply.

"Apologies. I've spoken out of turn and embarrassed you," he said.

"No, I . . . I simply wasn't expecting a declaration so soon." In all honesty, she was flummoxed by it. He hadn't seemed particularly devoted, but had given the impression he was constantly testing the waters regarding her suitability. "I do hold some affection for you, but I'm not yet to the point where I can commit myself . . . to anyone."

"Again, my apologies. You did not sit out a single dance. You had attention aplenty. I'm feeling a bit insecure and questioning my skills at wooing, as I've never before put them to the test."

She couldn't imagine Andrew feeling insecure about anything. If he was at all bothered by attention being given to a woman he fancied, she suspected he'd react with jealousy. He'd assert himself and make it known the lady held his regard and was not available.

"I have more competition now that your sister's fortunes have changed," Somerdale continued.

He was referring to the overlooking of Tillie's scandalous past. "She never should have been considered a *notorious heiress* to begin with." The unkind moniker had been attributed to her sister ever since she'd been spied kissing a footman. Few knew it had been a ruse to force her husband to divorce her.

"Perhaps not, but her actions were rather . . . untoward. I mean no offense, of course, but I seem to have gotten myself into a pickle here."

She hadn't helped matters by putting him on the spot. Rather ungracious of her. She gave him a soft smile. "Don't be concerned with the other gents. I'll not forget you took me rowing when everyone else was barely acknowledging me."

"I shall take comfort in knowing I have a leg up," he said as he started forward. "And what of Lord Andrew Mabry?"

"Pardon?"

"I noticed you waltzed with him last night."

Had everyone taken note of her partners? It was to be expected, she supposed, if a gentleman had a keen interest in her. "As you've already pointed out, I danced with a good many gents."

"Yes, but you never took your gaze from Mabry's. It was quite intense—the manner in which the two of you looked at each other. It made me wonder if you might welcome his suit."

"I walked down the aisle in the church with him as well, but that doesn't mean we're to marry. Besides, he is not of a mind to wed."

"Many a man not of a mind to wed finds himself at the altar."

Not Andrew. And certainly not with her. If he had not

kissed her when they were in such close proximity in that small room at the brothel or when they were so near when he delivered her to the door, he obviously had the fortitude to resist all temptation where she was concerned, while she would gladly surrender to it.

She tried to envision herself feeling as comfortable with Somerdale at a brothel, but the images simply wouldn't form. She couldn't see him not objecting when she went off with a dove, laughing when he realized all she'd been doing was conversing, encouraging her to peep at a couple who were on the precipice of fornicating.

She also realized that while she knew exactly how many—and precisely which—ladies Andrew had escorted onto the dance floor, she hadn't noticed if Somerdale had danced with anyone other than herself. He was kind, polite, loyal—all wonderful attributes—but they didn't make her grow warm with longing. Shouldn't she want more from a man than pleasant walks?

"I seem to have killed our conversation," he said with an awkward laugh.

"I was simply noticing the clouds. They seem to be growing darker. I think it's going to rain."

"We should probably start back then. You are as sweet as sugar and likely to melt if you get wet."

He was trying so hard to charm her. She felt rather badly that she wasn't charmed. Still, she patted his arm. "Yes, we probably should."

It was an odd thing. She'd wanted so desperately to be courted. And now she was finding it dull. Last night had

spoiled her. She wasn't certain if she'd ever again find anything as exciting.

Damn it all to hell! What the devil was Gina doing here, in
a secluded room at the Twin Dragons?

It was supposed to be a private card game with family and
close friends. Although Andrew supposed she now qualified as
both, at least in his sister's eyes. Grace sat beside Gina, leaning
toward her, showing her various cards, no doubt explaining the
rules of the game. He didn't know how much good the instructions were doing because Gina had not taken her gaze from
him since he'd stepped through the heavy draperies that separated the small gaming area from the sitting room behind him.

If he'd known she was going to be here, he'd have made his
excuses and searched for sport elsewhere, but he couldn't very
well leave now without having to offer some sort of explana-
tion for his abrupt departure. It wouldn't do at all to explain
he'd been in a constant state of arousal since delivering Gina
to his parents' residence the night before. He seemed incapable of purging her from his mind. Images of her sitting on the
bed with a molly, in the darkness peering into the forbidden,
and traveling demurely in his carriage fought for dominance,
each bringing with it some aspect of her that he never wanted
to forget.

"Why the frown, Andrew?" Lovingdon asked, watching
him as though horns were slowly sprouting from his forehead. As he'd abruptly developed a raging headache, perhaps
they were.

"I'm not frowning," he snapped. Was he? Good God, there was a time when he'd been able to keep all his emotions hidden behind a wall that suddenly seemed in danger of crumbling.

"Perhaps you're afraid I'll take all your money," Gina said.

He feared she might take something, but it had nothing to do with the coins in his purse. "Have you ever played before?" he asked, handing his jacket off to a footman, before beginning to roll up his sleeves while taking the only chair that remained available at the round table, one directly across from her.

She gave him a hesitant smile, but he noticed her eyes dipped to his arms as though she were fascinated by the simple task that revealed skin. "No, but I've had luck at the roulette table. Of course, your tutelage there helped."

"I wouldn't trust Andrew to do right by you when it comes to this game," Grace said. "He likes to win."

"We all like to win." He didn't know why he felt that tonight was some sort of test. "I assume this evening we'll be playing by guest rules."

"What are those?" Gina asked. "I don't want you to let me win."

"We're not that kind," he assured her. "We simply won't cheat."

Her smile grew, mesmerizing in its intensity. "Could you teach me to cheat?"

"It would require private lessons. I'm not going to reveal my methods to the scoundrels around this table." Which included the Dukes and Duchesses of Ashebury and Avendale. His family associated with far too many dukes.

"If you want to learn from an expert," Drake Darling, the owner of the establishment, said, "you'd be better off taking lessons from Grace. She's the most skilled."

Except Andrew didn't want her learning from Grace. If anyone was going to teach her anything at all, he wanted it to be him. Only what he really wanted to share with her were dark, forbidden things, things that if they were caught doing would bring censure down on them. He knew he shouldn't—couldn't—travel that path with her. She'd suffered through and survived her own sister's scandal without becoming cynical. She didn't need one of her own. It would change her irrevocably. He didn't want her any different than she was.

"Those instructions must wait for another night," Grace said. "Tonight we play honestly. Besides, it's good practice to do that every now and then, lest we forget how."

"Ante up," Drake announced.

Wooden chips were already sitting in front of Andrew. They always began the games with an equal amount, and Drake knew where to find each of them if they didn't pay up what they owed at the end. Andrew's parents had taken the street urchin in and raised him as one of their own. He was as much a brother to Andrew as Rex was.

He tossed a chip into the center of the table, watched as Gina did the same. Her small hands were bared. All their hands were bared. Made handling the cards easier. Sleeves were rolled past elbows so cards couldn't be hidden within them. Even though they were to play honestly tonight, he wasn't convinced everyone would adhere to the rule.

Without even signaling to a nearby footman, he found

himself with a glass of scotch, noticed Gina had a snifter of brandy. He'd have thought she'd have preferred wine. He wondered what else he might have guessed wrong about her. Wondered what he might have guessed right. Wondered anything and everything. It had been years since he'd given a fig about what pleasures a woman might offer outside the bed.

The last time he had, he'd been young, naïve, and in the end remarkably stupid. While he enjoyed the company of women immensely, he'd become the worst sort of miser, never again investing his heart or his soul in any relationship. Less chance for experiencing pain that way. Hence he understood Rex warning him away from Gina. She deserved someone who would embrace her wholeheartedly. Andrew would always hold himself in check where emotions were concerned. Having been burned badly once, he had no desire to suffer again.

The cards were dealt. After gathering his up, he lifted only the edges to see what he'd been dealt. Then he peered surreptitiously at Gina. A delicate pleat creased her brow. She glanced down at the list of winning combinations someone had written for her. He could fairly hear her squealing with joy inside her mind as her green eyes sparkled and her smile brightened. No one was going to have to cheat to beat her.

"Andrew, you're up," Lovingdon suddenly barked, causing Andrew to turn his attention back to his cards. "The bid is twenty quid."

"Has every aspect of the game been explained to Miss Hammersley?" he asked, striving for a boredom he wasn't feeling. He wondered if making love to her would garner the same excitement and enthusiasm on her part.

"You must call me Gina. We're related now. I'm practically a sister."

"I think the law only views you as related to Rex."

"When it comes to family, when have we ever taken into account how the law views relations?" Grace asked.

Since his body had begun having inappropriate reactions to Gina's nearness.

"I consider myself related by my heart to everyone at this table," she carried on, determined to make her point and make him feel like a total ass for a comment designed to remind himself that Gina was, in fact, *not* his sister. That the thoughts he had regarding her would not have him burning in hell. "Blood, marriage licenses, birth certificates really have no bearing on how I view those who mean the most—"

"Calling and raising thirty," he said, to get the game moving and his sister off her definition of family.

Avendale and his wife called. Lovingdon narrowed his eyes before folding. Grace tossed her chips onto the pile. Gina looked at the list again, gnawed on her lower lip. He wanted to nibble there, stroke his tongue over it, soothe it. His cock stirred as though he was doing precisely that. He shifted in the chair. It was going to be a long night.

Finally she gave a quick nod, like she'd convinced herself of something, gave him a sly grin, and slid her chips toward the pile, and he couldn't stop himself from imagining her sliding those fingers over his shoulders, his chest, lower . . . she'd be the death of him yet. "I'll call and raise you fifty. I can do that, can't I?"

She looked at him imploringly as though it would break

her heart if he said no. If she couldn't, he'd have said yes and changed the rules then and there to accommodate her desire. Bloody hell, what was wrong with him?

"You can," Grace told her, "but remember there is another round of betting after we exchange cards."

"I remember."

Drake sat beside her. He wasn't playing, merely dealing. He may have told Gina that Grace was the best at cheating, but the truth was: he was the best of the lot. So even when no cheating was to take place, he wasn't allowed to play with them because his sleight of hand bordered on the divine. Although he didn't always use his skill to benefit himself. Andrew wondered what cards he might have slipped to Gina.

"That's a bit rich for me," Ashebury said, tossing down his cards. His wife, Minerva, carelessly flipped some tokens to the center of the table.

Andrew tapped his finger on the table, peered at his pair of jacks. He considered stretching out his leg and kicking Drake to see if he could get him to give some subtle signal regarding what Gina might be holding. His brother might own an establishment that catered to the vices, but Drake was one of the most generous souls he'd ever known. He wouldn't allow Gina's first experience to be disappointing. Although perhaps he was expecting everyone else to be sporting about it. "I'll accept your raise . . ."

He picked up the necessary chips, tapped them on the table, found himself dragging out the moment because the anticipation in her eyes gave him a small measure of satisfaction, made him want to keep her attention, made him want to see her anticipating other things, carnal things. He flicked the wooden chips onto the others, allowing the clacking of wood to break the spell. ". . . and leave it at that."

Drake began exchanging cards with the other players. Andrew was well aware, however, that his brother's attention was more riveted on him than his actions, as though he were striving to decipher some puzzle. He tossed back his scotch, signaled for more.

Gina asked for only two cards. He wondered if she was holding three of a kind. That would beat his jacks. But what if she held three different face cards and was hoping for a pair? What if he took the win? What if he was the one who caused her joy in the game to diminish?

"Andrew?" Drake asked, a question in his voice that went beyond needing to know how many cards he wanted.

While it went against the grain and his competitive nature, he tossed away three cards, one of them the jack of hearts. "Three."

He nearly burst out laughing when he saw the ten and two jacks that he'd received in return. He'd have had a bloody four of a kind. Never in all the games he'd played, all the ways he'd cheated, had he ever had that wondrous hand land in his lap. Three jacks, though, could still very well beat her.

When the bet came to him, he met Minerva's fifty and raised a hundred. That knocked the Duchess of Avendale out. Grace folded. Gina was gnawing her lip again, but he could sense the excitement in her. If she wasn't sitting, she'd no doubt be dancing around on her toes, spinning about.

"I shall call and raise another hundred," she said.

Minerva folded. He looked at Drake, who gave him a very subtle shake of his head. Did that mean fold or not? Did it signal she had something or she didn't? "Call. Show me your cards."

Three queens. Thank God.

He revealed his hand. When she gave him a smile so bright that it nearly blinded him, he was glad he hadn't folded. He was willing to lose every round to her for that smile.

Antes were made. As the next set of cards were dealt, Minerva said, "I suppose we should have invited Somerdale."

"Why the devil would we do that?" Andrew asked, waiting to peer at his cards because he believed it was bad luck to look too early. Gina, on the other hand, picked each one up as it landed in front of her, her smile growing with each card added.

"Because I saw him at the park with Gina. He's courting you, isn't he?" she asked with a pointed look. "Quite seriously it appears."

"Quite determinedly," Gina admitted, briefly looking away from her cards, her smile softening as though she had fond memories of the bloke and his courtship skills.

"Do you fancy him, then?" the Duchess of Avendale asked.

"I do. When everyone else was giving me a wide berth, he took me rowing."

Rowing? How boring. He could think of a dozen ways to entertain her that would prove more exciting than sitting in a boat. Might as well be sitting in a parlor.

"He didn't seem at all embarrassed to be seen with me,"

she continued. "His previous kindness does give him a leg up over the others."

"The others?" Andrew bit back a curse at the tone of his voice. The words had come out accusingly.

She angled her head, studying him thoughtfully, and he felt rather like a dog that had been caught chewing the master's shoe. "Yes, four other gentlemen called on me this afternoon."

Before he could demand to know who they were, Grace said, "You should have seen all the flowers in the residence when we arrived to invite Gina to join us. I daresay, at least half a dozen gents are keen to let it be known they, too, will be calling. And to think: we were all so busy assisting with the arrangements for Rex's hasty marriage that we've barely begun our campaign to see her betrothed by Season's end."

"Why set deadlines on something that should come about naturally?" he asked.

"Fifty," Ashebury announced.

"Call," Minerva responded.

"Well, because having a goal helps one to stay focused," Grace said. "Surely during all your travels you find you make better use of your time if you have a list of the places you wish to tour."

He was rather certain she didn't mean to make it sound as though he had no worthwhile goals to speak of, that he was more concerned with play, but he couldn't help but feel a measure of judgment in her words. He was the second son. He was given an allowance. His life was one of carefree ease.

"Call or fold, Andrew," Drake said.

"Call. A list of the brothels and taverns I wish to visit is helpful."

"Don't take offense because I worry you may do nothing useful with your life."

"I intend to do something very useful: I'm going to take every chip stacked before you." Then, because he knew she wasn't the only one at the table who saw him as a wastrel, he tossed back his scotch and signaled for more.

"Don't you start cheating," Grace commanded.

"Wouldn't dream of it." But he would do it if Gina weren't there.

He didn't take Grace's chips that hand, Minerva did. The next two hands everyone folded because Gina's smile was so sunny.

The next round saw him with three aces. In spite of Gina's pleased expression, he doubted she could best him. He had a moment of doubt when she exchanged only one card—until her face fell when she saw what she'd been given. He wagered a hundred. She folded.

"Show me what you had," he said.

She tilted up that pert little nose of hers. "Show me what you had."

"I don't have to. You folded."

"Since I did, I don't have to show you anything."

"But you can't learn to play well if you get no instruction at all. Show me."

She gave him a pointed glare. He tossed down his cards, face up.

"Oh," she said. "I was wise to fold." She turned over her cards. Four, five, six, eight.

"Never draw to an inside straight," he told her. "The odds are against you."

"They're always against you."

"But more so in that instance." Reaching across the table, placing his hand behind her ear, he brought it forward and flicked a seven of clubs at her.

She released a tiny squeal. "How did you do that?"

"It's one of the cards I discarded."

"But where did you hide it? Your sleeves are rolled up."

"How I managed it is of no consequence. What matters is that it was no longer in the deck when you were in need of a seven. I need to stretch my legs. Come with me."

Grace furrowed her brow. "What are you up to, Andrew?"

Gina smiled. "You're going to teach me to cheat, aren't you?"

He chuckled. "No, but I am planning to teach you something."

"You will behave," Grace admonished.

"Dear Sister, why would I not?"

She exchanged a questioning look with Minerva, as though they both thought him up to no good.

"She's safe with me," he said curtly, irritated the words needed to be voiced aloud, more irritated that he wasn't absolutely sure they were completely true.

When he and Gina were out in the hallway, she asked quietly, "Are you going to give me a lesson like you did last night?"

"No." Fighting not to think of last night, he escorted her to the balcony that looked out over the gaming floor.

She wandered to the edge, peered down. "I love the sounds. Very different from those made in a brothel. I found myself contemplating them several times today."

"Don't."

Turning slightly, she studied him. "Don't . . . ?"

"We're not here to discuss past adventures."

"Then why are we here? Is there another adventure you'd like to take me on?"

One between the sheets. He shoved that image back into the corner of his mind. "Have you noticed how often people are folding in there?"

"Indeed, yes. They must not be receiving decent cards."

"You telegraph with your facial expressions when you've received what you believe will be a winning hand."

"I do?"

Placing his hand on her waist, he urged her into the shadows. He skimmed his fingers over her eyebrows. They were darker than her hair, with a delicate arch to them. "You raise your eyebrows just a tad."

He glided his forefinger along her temple, down to her cheek. "Your eyes sparkle like emeralds reflecting sunlight."

They weren't sparkling now, though. They were warming with pleasure as she stared into his eyes. He dropped his hand farther, stroked his thumb over her full, lower lip, felt the tiniest of quivers run through her. "Your smile is one of pure satisfaction."

Her pink tongue darted out, dampened the pad of his

thumb. His stomach tightened, his cock twitched. He touched the corner of her mouth and shoved out the next words. "And when you don't get the card you need, you frown." His voice sounded rough and raw. "You telegraph your pleasure or displeasure with the cards. You don't want to give that information to your competitors."

"What should I do?" she rasped.

Ask me to kiss you. "Keep your face still. Don't smile. Don't take delight in the cards." He trailed his finger along her throat. So silky, so smooth. Down. Then up to where her pulse beat furiously. "Imagine me kissing you."

"Would that not delight me?" Her voice was breathy, low, sensual. It fit the shadows, was suited to bed play. He wanted it near his ear as he rode her.

"It would, but thinking about it would serve as a distraction, would put distance between you and the cards."

"Is that how you manage not to give anything away? By imagining kissing me?"

"Oh, I imagine a good deal more than that."

She licked her lips. If Somerdale ever tasted them, he might have to plow his fist into the man's face.

"Having never been kissed," she rasped, "I can't quite conjure what I should imagine. Perhaps you should demonstrate."

How had he come to this moment of doing something he knew was totally and absolutely wrong? Not a single person sitting at the table in that private room would approve. His parents would disapprove mightily. Rex would not only take him to task, he was likely to bloody Andrew's nose. Yet knowing it would be frowned upon, was forbidden, would identify him as a cad of the lowest order, he couldn't find the will to resist.

Not when her eyes were searching his, not when her lips parted slightly, not when she lifted her mouth as an offering, a sacrifice, a surrendering.

He glanced down the hallway. Empty. He guided her farther into the shadows, cradled the underside of her jaw, felt the pulse at her throat thundering against his fingertips. Certain he could school her in the art of a kiss without involving anything more than his mouth, he lowered it to hers.

The plumpness of her lips welcomed him like the softest of pillows; the warmth hit him like the sun on a summer afternoon when he was stretched out over a bed of clover. Her hushed sigh was the sweetest lullaby ever sung.

Without prompting she opened her mouth to him and he was lost, lost to the glorious taste and heat of her, the velvet and silk of her tongue gliding over his. One of her hands folded around his upper arm, the other clasped the back of his neck, her fingers scraping up into his hair. He snaked his free arm around her back, crushed her to him.

God help him. Kissing her was more marvelous than he'd imagined. Every breath he took only served to bring a deeper awareness of her violet fragrance. With each sweep of his tongue, he tasted brandy darkened by her enjoyment of it. Her mouth was paradise and decadence.

And not enough. Not nearly enough.

He wanted to peel off the layers of her clothes and feast on her flesh, raining kisses over every inch, circling his tongue around her nipples—would they be pink or dark, small or large? He wanted to draw the tiny buds into his mouth and suckle until she was writhing against him, wrapping her legs tightly around his hips and holding on for dear life.

He wanted everything he could not have, should not have, would not have.

A kiss, this moment, was all the indulgence he could spare. She was not the sort with whom a man toyed. She was the type a man married. She was an incredibly wealthy heiress who could have her pick of men: titled lords, princes, and kings. Not second sons, not *spares* who were expected to never amount to anything of importance.

He drew back. She blinked as though awakening from a dream, her eyes glazed over. Touching his thumb to her damp and swollen lips, he wanted to taste them again, wanted to take her someplace where he could taste them more thoroughly.

"We've been gone too long." His voice sounded as though he'd been a month without drink.

She merely nodded.

"Are you all right?" he asked quietly.

Again a nod. "It was more involved than I expected it to be."

"Not nearly as involved as it could have been. Think about that. Let it distract you so you don't show any emotion whatsoever at the cards you're dealt."

He escorted her back to the room. Everyone was standing around, drinking and talking. As he pulled out the chair for Gina, the others began taking their seats.

"You were gone a rather long time," Grace said, with suspicion.

"If you must know, I was providing her with some tips. She's giving too much away."

"Oh." She seemed surprised by his answer.

"What else would I have been doing?"

"You're a young buck, she's a young lady." She arched a brow at him.

"You're a suspicious wench. She's family now. I wouldn't take advantage."

"See that you don't." She lowered herself onto the chair.

He winked at Gina. She gave him a warm smile. He did wish he didn't like it so much. "Remember what I taught you," he said sternly, hoping to give the impression that nothing untoward had happened while they'd been absent from the room.

"I assure you I shall never forget."

He suspected she wasn't referring to his counsel regarding the need to keep a straight face when playing cards. Three hands later he was rather certain of it because she showed continual delight with the cards she was dealt, completely ignoring his advice. His demonstration had been a waste—

That was untrue. Nothing in his life had ever been less a waste. Nor so unwise. He could still taste her on his tongue, and that kept him in a continual state of distraction. But she was as happy as a lark with her latest hand. Everyone else had folded. It was left to him to call or fold. He'd already put three hundred into the pot. She wanted five hundred more.

She was waiting expectantly, beaming as though she'd found her heart's desire beneath the tree on Christmas morning. He peered at his two queens. She had to be holding something better. A wise man knew when to cut his losses. "Fold."

With a victorious smile, she laid down her cards and began collecting her winnings.

"So what did you have?" he asked.

Stopping, she met his gaze. "You'll never know. You weren't willing to pay for the privilege of seeing them."

"Because you looked so bloody cheerful. I advised you to keep your emotions in check."

"As I'm the one gathering up the chips, perhaps I didn't need your advice."

Suspicion roiling through him, he scowled. "I want to see your cards."

"No."

"You're new to the game. If you show us what you had, what you threw away, we can help you determine best how to win."

"I'm already winning."

Before she could react, he lunged across the table and snatched up her cards. She shrieked and reached for them, but he held them aloft until he could get a good look at them. He flung them onto the table. "You had nothing."

"I had five cards."

"But none of them matched in any way. None of them amounted to anything. You were grinning like a loon— bloody hell. You show excitement no matter what you have."

"While I realize you lot fold quite a bit, I still get the take, even if it isn't very much. Small amounts eventually add up to large amounts."

He barked out his laughter. "You swindler! How many hands have you had nothing?"

She shrugged, an impish smile spreading over her face. "I can't recall."

"So there is a method to your madness."

"I don't fancy how serious you all look. So I thought if I always smile, you'll always think I have something of value." Placing her elbows on the table, she leaned forward. "I will wager five hundred quid right this minute that you were holding at least a pair. Probably face cards, but I'm not wagering on that. Only the pair. Prove me wrong. Show me what you had."

He could think of things to show her that had nothing at all to do with cards. He glanced around the table. Everyone else seemed to be waiting on bated breath. "I'd be a fool to accept your wager."

With a flick of his wrist, he turned over his cards. The two queens mocked him.

Dear God, but she was beautiful when victorious. "How did you know?"

"You tap the table with your forefinger when you think you're holding cards that will beat the others."

"I always tap the table."

"Yes, but when you don't have anything you use all your fingers."

"She's right," Grace crowed. "How clever you are, Gina, to spot his habit so quickly."

"You were aware I did that?" he asked. Even he hadn't been cognizant of it.

Grace didn't have the decency to look abashed. "Why do you think I always beat you?"

"Because you manipulate the cards."

"I have to figure out what you're holding in order to determine how best to manipulate them."

He shifted his gaze back to Gina. "Perhaps we should step into the hallway and you can give me some lessons on how not to give anything away."

He wanted to reach across the table and flatten his palm against the blush warming her cheeks.

"I think there have been enough lessons for tonight," Grace said. "And enough gaming. We should be off."

"Afraid I'm ready to call it a night as well," Minerva said.

"Same here," Avendale announced.

"Which is why I shall never marry," Andrew said. "Marriage breeds boredom. You all serve as perfect examples. It's not even nine." He looked at Gina. "If you wish to stay longer, spend some time on the gaming floor, I'll escort you home."

"That might be viewed as inappropriate," Grace said. "You're a bachelor. Hardly chaperone material."

"You're the one who said we were family."

"Still, we must protect her reputation."

"I could send word to my maid to join me here," Gina said. "If I'm on the gaming floor until she arrives, everyone will know I did nothing untoward. Then if Andrew would be kind enough to see us both home . . . I really would like to stay a bit longer."

Grace looked at her husband, who merely shrugged. She glanced over at Minerva.

"I don't see the harm," the Duchess of Ashebury said. "Besides, spending time on the gaming floor would probably serve her courtship goals better than being hidden away in here with us. One of the nice things about the Dragons is that it provides a social environment outside of the ballrooms."

"You're right. I'm probably just being overprotective," Grace said. She gave him a hard look. "Have her home by midnight. I promised Mother. You know how she worries until all the chicks are home."

With good reason. Her chicks tended to do things they ought not, especially when temptation came in such a lovely package as Gina Hammersley did.

Oh she was a wicked girl. She hadn't wanted to go to the gaming floor. She'd wanted to find a dark quiet place where Andrew could bestow another kiss upon her.

But Grace had escorted her to the roulette wheel before she and her husband had departed. Now she had the attention of two other gentlemen—she'd been introduced to them recently, had danced with one at the wedding ball—and knew she should be grateful for it, should relish it, but couldn't seem to keep her attention on either gent.

Instead she was constantly looking over to where Andrew stood at a table throwing dice. She loved the way he shook the ivory, released the cubes, then looked over the heads of the people bending to see what he'd thrown and met her gaze. Even from this distance, she could see the heat in his.

"You won again, Miss Hammersley," Lord Manville said, turning her attention back to him.

"So I did." She gathered up her winnings, placed another wager.

"Will you be at the Waverly ball?" he asked.

She smiled at him. "Those are my plans."

"Excellent. I should like to go ahead and claim your first dance."

"I'll take the second," the other gent, Lord Benson, said.

Laughing gently, she felt the heat rise in her cheeks. From the moment the Season had begun she'd longed for such attention, but now there was only one gent with whom she wished to dance. "Duly noted. I shall live in anticipation of the ball's arrival."

And the evening's end. The gentlemen were charming, but they didn't make her wonder what they were thinking, what sort of mischief they might get up to once they left the Dragons. She wondered if she might be able to convince Andrew to take her with him again. Surely he engaged in activities beyond wagering and *brotheling*. Was that even a word? It should be. It sounded much less harsh than the one Venus had taught her for the sexual act.

Her heart gave a little kick as Andrew strode toward her. She was barely aware of the ball bouncing over the roulette wheel, landing, the cheers going up, and the congratulations on another win being offered to her. Her focus was entirely on him.

"You seem to be having luck," he said once he reached her.

She wanted that luck to continue, only with him. "It seems so, yes."

He leaned in. "I've yet to see your maid arrive."

She rolled her eyes and whispered, "I forgot to send for her."

A corner of his mouth hitched up. "I thought you might. As it's late, I should probably escort you home now."

"As we're family," she said a little louder, "I'm sure no one will think anything of that." While she said good night to the gentlemen surrounding her, Andrew gathered up her winnings, saw to it that her chips were exchanged for currency. Her reticule was considerably heavier as they walked toward the door. "If you're heading off on an adventure, I want to go with you," she announced boldly, but low enough that no one else would hear.

"Only off to bed." Then to her surprise and delight, he blushed. "And you are most certainly not going with me."

Pity. "What about tomorrow night?"

"What about it?"

"There isn't a ball until the night after. What am I to do with myself until then?"

"Oh I'm certain Grace will come up with some sort of entertainment for you."

A footman opened the door. She and Andrew walked out into the night.

"Will you be at the Waverly ball? Manville and Benson already claimed dances. My card is likely to fill rather quickly. I'll happily save a dance for you."

"I won't be attending."

She was surprised by how her enthusiasm for the Waverly affair suddenly dimmed. Perhaps if she spoke with the duchess, she'd convince her son to go. Although it was probably best if he didn't. She found it difficult to give attention to anyone when he was about. If she wanted to be betrothed by the end of the Season, she needed to set her mind to it.

Although it was dark, except for the occasional street lamp, Andrew ran, barefoot, through the park near his town house. His body was in mortal danger of exploding, and he needed to do something to exhaust himself so he could sleep. He'd hated watching all the gents fawning over Gina. Not that she didn't deserve fawning over, but still it had irritated.

Traveling with her in the carriage, inhaling her fragrance of violets, had been pure torment. He'd wanted to cross over to her, gather her up in his arms, and kiss her silly.

It had been a mistake to kiss her earlier. He'd been downing whiskey, striving to rid himself of her flavor, and he couldn't do it. It was as though her taste had taken up permanent residence in his mouth. No woman had ever affected him as she did.

He wished he had a heart to offer her, but years ago it had been shattered. No matter how hard he tried, he could not seem to put it back together.

CHAPTER 7

Gina sat at the pianoforte and played a haunting melody that caused her to feel a bit melancholy, when she knew no reason existed for such morose sentiments. No balls, dinners, or soirees were taking place tonight—at least none to which she'd been invited. The duke and duchess had retired for the evening, encouraging her to make herself at home. She tried reading, but it was simply too quiet. She was rather glad Tillie had insisted she not return to Landsdowne Court. Even with the servants about, she'd still find only loneliness there.

A hand appeared before her, reaching for the music sheets. With a tiny screech, she stopped playing and twisted about to stare up at Andrew. He was so near she could see the tiny ring of black that circled the light blue of his eyes, could smell bergamot and lemon and something much darker, an indulgence. Whiskey or brandy or a very rich wine.

"What are you doing here?" The question was inane. This residence belonged to his parents. He no doubt came and went with frequent regularity.

With his back to the piano, he lowered himself to the bench, his hip resting against hers. In spite of her petticoats, she felt the firmness and warmth. "I noticed you weren't at the Twin Dragons so I thought Grace might have abandoned you for the night and you might be in need of relief from your boredom. Nothing against my parents, but they can become quite dull as the evening progresses."

"Another outing to the Twin Dragons?"

"I had something else in mind."

Rowing, at night. She'd never considered it possible, wondered if her remarks about Somerdale taking her rowing had influenced him at all. It was cooler here; he'd wrapped her in a blanket and she snuggled down into it.

The full moon as well as a lantern suspended from the bow of the small boat guided them along the river. She didn't think they were on the Thames, didn't really know where they were, didn't care. Instead she absorbed the peace and tranquility of the water gently lapping against the boat, the slap of the oars, the splash of a fish. The quiet of the man sitting across from her.

It was odd that when she was with him, she didn't need conversation. When she was with others, she always felt she was being judged—her dress, her manners, her mien, her refinement. Were any of them proper enough to gain her a husband? What if she were poor? Would she spend her life alone? Wealth was a pitfall that lead to insecurities and complications when it shouldn't.

"Somerdale called on me this afternoon." He groaned. Perhaps from the strain of rowing, although she didn't think so. "As did Manville and Wheatley."

"Seems you have a virtual cornucopia of suitors."

He sounded displeased which pleased her. "Have you ever courted a woman?"

"I have no plans to marry."

Which wasn't exactly an answer to the question. "I know I've asked before but you didn't give a very succinct answer: Have you ever been in love?"

"Again, no plans to marry."

She frowned. "You can love without marrying. What about your actress? Surely you cared for her."

"Immensely, but I did not love her, nor did she love me. We were together because we enjoyed each other's company."

She couldn't imagine the actress hadn't fallen in love with him just a little. "Did you make her laugh?"

"On occasion. What has that to do with anything?"

"Tillie says you can't really love someone who doesn't make you laugh. Or at least, you shouldn't marry someone who doesn't make you laugh."

"Does Somerdale make you laugh?"

She shook her head. "No. I like him well enough, but he's trying too hard to win me over. It seems love should come about more naturally, more of a slow awakening, a realization he's the one you want to clasp your hand when it's wrinkled and frail and you're old. Your parents hold hands. They touch often: a shoulder, an arm, the small of the back. I can tell they do it without thinking. That's the sort of love I want. One that doesn't require any thinking."

"If you never think about it, you can take it for granted."

"For someone who avoids love, you seem to have considerable knowledge regarding it. Who broke your heart?"

She could feel him studying her. Limned by moonlight as he was, his silhouette was clearly visible but she couldn't detect the subtleties in his facial expressions. They were lost to the shadows. Rubbing her hands, she realized she might have pushed a bit too far. "It's chilly out here."

"Is the blanket not warding off the cold?"

"It's helping some." She was also wearing a pelisse he'd told her to bring. But there was a slight breeze that wanted to work itself into the very marrow of her bones.

She watched as he took the oars from the water and set them along the sides of the skiff. Shoving himself off the bench, he settled into the bottom of the boat and held out his hand. "Come here."

Her heart fluttered as she took his hand, slid onto her knees, turned around, and wedged herself between his legs, her back to his chest. He brought up the sides of his coat and she snuggled in deeper against the heat provided by his body. "Oh, that's lovely. It's always so much more rewarding to be warmed after I'm cold. I appreciate it more."

"Mmm." His voice was a low thrum near her ear and the bristles lining his jaw brushed enticingly against her cheek. He closed his bare hands around her gloved ones, and additional warmth seeped into her being.

"Tell me about her," she demanded softly.

"Gina—"

"I know there was someone. Perhaps you didn't love her, perhaps she didn't break your heart, but you don't learn to avoid the fire until you've been burned. And you must admit you have an aversion to love. I won't tell a soul. Your secrets are always safe with me, Andrew."

"I can't be the only one revealing secrets. If I answer, you must share with me the most intimate thing you've ever done with a man. And if our kiss last night is your answer, then you must tell me the most intimate thing you've ever imagined doing."

The fog was rolling in, and she couldn't help but think it was taking all the air with it as she was having a frightfully difficult time drawing in a breath. She nodded—no doubt unwisely. "I accept your terms."

His arms closed more securely around her, wrapping her in a cocoon of heat.

"When I was nineteen," he began quietly, "I met a woman, two years' my senior, who intrigued me as no other female had. I'd yet to take an interest in balls, debutantes, or courtship but for her I recited Browning's poems and Shakespeare's sonnets, wrote poetry, sang ballads. I was quite . . . smitten."

Not as strong a word as *love* and she wondered if he had an aversion to the term and experiencing the emotion. "How did you meet?"

"Our paths crossed when I was riding in the park. She caught my attention. Actually, her smile caught my attention. If ever a painting were created to demonstrate a come-hither look, hers would have served as the example."

"Was she pretty?"

"Beautiful. While it was a bold action, I introduced myself. She hinted she would be visiting a particular museum the following day—at two—and I made a point to be there. She was alone. Our first kiss occurred behind the statue of a scantily clad couple lost in an embrace."

"You certainly recall the particulars." She didn't like the jealousy that speared her.

"I remember everything. Every encounter. Every stolen moment. Her reputation needed to remain untarnished. She wanted no scandal—much like you. And nothing at all like you."

The last was said so quietly she almost didn't hear it.

"As I mentioned I was nineteen. Still residing with my parents. I wanted to be completely alone with her. I wanted more than kisses. She yearned for them as well. There is a club for those who seek secretive trysts."

"The Nightingale Club," she offered. "I've heard of it."

His breath wafted over her cheek. "I assume you've never been."

"Absolutely not. But I've wondered about it. If it's as decadent as they say."

"More so. It is a refuge for sinners and when you are surrounded by those desiring what you desire, it is easy to forget the wrongness of it."

"But still, you met her there."

"I did. As often as I could. I fell in love with her there. I decided I would make an honest woman of her. I would court her properly."

"What did she say when you told her?"

"I didn't tell her. I sought to surprise her. So I began to attend balls. At the third one, I spied her, standing with a group of men and women. But I didn't really see them. I saw only her. The besotted fool I was, I rushed over to greet her, to let her know I was there, to ask for a dance. I knew the moment she spotted me. She didn't smile or appear to be happy to see me. She showed no emotion whatsoever, as though her features had been frozen in ice. When I finally arrived, with my heart pounding, she merely said, 'Hello, Lord Andrew.' And then she introduced me to her husband."

She twisted around. "You didn't know she was married?"

"No, I knew only her Christian name. Unlike Rex, who was continually expected to attend social functions and was introduced to this lord and that, who accompanied Father when he went to his clubs so he would know who was powerful and who was not, who was a political ally, who might be an enemy, I was left to wander about wherever I wanted. I wasn't bothered by my father's ignoring of me. I had no interest in meetings, in learning what I must know in order to one day take over the reins. They would not be handed to me. I much preferred learning where the best whiskey was served, the more interesting wagering took place, and the most willing women were to be found."

"What did you do when confronted with her husband?"

"I did what any good whore does: I pretended she meant nothing to me and it was a pleasure to meet him."

She could hear the disgust in his voice—disgust with himself. The woman had made him feel less, feel used. She couldn't imagine it, the bruising his pride must have taken. "The woman didn't deserve you."

"Her words were very similar when we met up later on an upper floor balcony, in the darkness away from everyone. 'Spares are for fucking,' she said. 'Not for marrying.'"

While she might not know who the woman was, she felt an immediate gut reaction to her: she hated her. Not out of jealousy because the beastly creature had held Andrew's affection—although she feared that might be part of it—but because the lady had hurt him, used such ugly words to describe her association with him. "She was a horrid woman. What she said wasn't true. A goodly number of second sons marry."

He chuckled darkly. "Not this one."

"Who was she?"

"It doesn't matter."

"Of course it matters. If I don't know who she is then how am I to tear out her hair from her head."

His laugh was low, dark, soothing. She felt him relax against her. Until that moment she hadn't realized how tense he'd been sharing something so personal with her. His lips, warmer than usual, landed below her ear, threatened to melt her where she sat.

"You're a temptress. You tempt in me in so many ways that you shouldn't, to confess things best left as secrets, to do things best not done."

"I'm glad you told me."

"I don't know why I did. I've never told anyone else."

"And the things best left undone? What would they in-volve?"

His hand came around, cradled her cheek, tilted her head back slightly. Then his mouth blanketed hers. There was no longer any chill, any breeze, any rocking motion on the water. There was only him.

He didn't know what had possessed him to blather on about something he'd fought so hard to forget, but she made him feel as though he could tell her anything, made him want to tell her everything—including the one thing he could never tell her: how much he'd come to care for her.

She was an heiress with a fortune, could have any man she wanted, deserved a titled gentleman with vast estates—not the second son who would never amount to anything. Although for her, he might be willing to put his playful ways behind him. For her, he didn't want to contemplate all he might do. Or how difficult it might be.

Because at that very moment he was having to refrain from doing all he wanted to do. As his tongue swept through her mouth, as she welcomed him, as her fingers became en-tangled in his hair, he wanted to possess her fully, wanted to caress every aspect of her body. He wanted her to palm his bollocks, stroke his cock. He wanted to fill her—without a sheath. To have an experience with her that he'd never had with another. He wanted to feel the slickness of her muscles closing around him, coaxing his seed to burst forth.

Christ! He certainly couldn't do that. He tore his mouth from hers, gazed into her limpid eyes. She was so beautiful, even when the night shadows prevented him from seeing her clearly.

"We should no doubt head back." His voice was embarrassingly rough and raw. He hoped all her petticoats prevented her from being aware of his throbbing erection. Usually, he was better able to control his reaction to a woman. But she unmanned him.

"I suppose we should."

He assisted her in returning to her bench, taking delight in her small squeal when the boat rocked unsteadily, but then he took delight in everything about her. Once he was settled, he grabbed the oars and began rowing. He had a great deal of pent-up energy to unleash.

They returned to shore in short order. He disembarked, pulled the skiff partway onto land, and held out his hand to her. She placed hers in it, rose. The boat wobbled.

"Easy now," he cooed.

She moved forward, the skiff rocked more precariously. She screeched, released her hold on him, threw up her arms for balance—

And over she went.

CHAPTER 8

He rescued her.

She was a wicked, wicked girl because she'd known he would, and she'd wanted him to. As firm and steady as his hold on her had been, she could have easily made it to shore, but she wasn't ready for her night with him to come to a close. She wasn't ready to admit that nothing profound had transpired between them when he'd told his tale. She wasn't ready to pretend she didn't care for him.

And she'd known he couldn't deliver her, looking like a drowned cat, to his parents' home. What if they'd awakened and were roaming the hallways? What if a servant caught sight of her? Her reputation would be left in shambles.

She'd explained all this to him as she sat in his carriage with his coat draped over her shoulders.

"I can sneak you in," he said to her now.

"If my clothing were dry, it would be so much easier. Wet, my shoes squeak when I walk."

He gazed out the window as though the answer resided

beyond the confines of the conveyance. "I don't have a lady's maid who could assist you."

"You must have some female servant."

"I never see them."

"Is your home dusty? Are your floors unpolished? Is your bed each night exactly as unkempt as it was when you left it that morning?"

"Of course not."

"Then you have at least one female servant. She will suffice to assist me in laying my clothes before a fire and tidying my hair."

She thought she heard him mutter, "Dangerous."

"It shouldn't take long," she persisted. "I'd be mortified for your parents to see me in such a state, to know I'm so clumsy."

He blew out an audible breath, before shouting up instructions to the driver. They were going to his residence. She kept her smile small, hopefully invisible to him, but deep down inside her, where dreams resided, she was frolicking.

She was in his residence, in a bedchamber, being assisted by a maid when he dearly wanted to assist her in loosening buttons, freeing laces, unknotting ribbons. Instead he stood by the fire in his small library, downing scotch. He'd changed out of his wet clothing—quickly because the temptation of her so near was almost too much for a normal man to resist, and nearly impossible for one as randy as he was.

Taking her rowing at night had been a stupid thing. He'd

been jealous of Somerdale—Somerdale for God's sake. Jealous, which was even worse. He was not prone to jealousy. Early on he'd learned that in any relationship he was better served to retain a measure of distance when it came to his heart. But he'd wanted to give her an experience on the water that put Somerdale's to shame.

He'd gone to the private room at the Dragons expecting her to be there. When he saw that she wasn't, he hadn't wanted to stay. So he'd made hasty arrangements for tonight's outing. Again, stupid. It was as though he had very little control over his actions, and most assuredly not over any rational thought process. Of late, all wisdom seemed to have fled.

He never spent much time in his residence. Most of the furnishings and the few decorations had been chosen by his mother or Grace, and they'd provided little, assuming at some point a wife would finish things off. No one seemed to expect him to hold to his vow of never marrying.

If he were honest, Gina often made him question the wisdom of it. He liked variety in his women, but became quickly bored. He doubted he'd ever become bored with her.

He thought he'd been concentrating on the fire, but he must have been watching for her out of the corner of his eye, because he was immediately aware of her stepping into the room in bare feet, a blanket draped over her, held tightly to her breast. If she were wearing nothing at all beneath it, he was going to be in terrible trouble.

"I hope you don't mind," she said quietly, almost shyly, "but I borrowed one of your shirts."

Even worse. Imagining the way it would swallow her up,

he found himself jealous of a bit of linen. And as he'd already proven, when jealousy was involved, he lost any ability to reason. "Would you care for some brandy to warm you up a bit more?"

She smiled. "Yes, please."

While he saw to pouring her a drink, she padded over to one of the two chairs in front of the fire, sat, and tucked her feet up beneath her. He could see a knee peeking out from a part in the blanket. Torture had a new name and it was Gina.

He refilled his own glass to the brim with whiskey before walking over and handing her the snifter. He did wish she didn't look so grateful, so alluring, so damned provocative. He was on a very short tether here, strained and taut, that was likely to snap at any moment.

He dropped into his chair, took two quick gulps of the oaky liquid, a third gulp for good measure. If he were a gentleman, he'd alert her to the rebelliousness of her knee and suggest she cover it. Apparently, he was not. His mother would be sorely disappointed in him. Later, much later, when he was fifty, he would no doubt be sorely disappointed in himself as well. Not so much at seventy. He had little doubt he'd still remember that knee and be grateful for the memory.

"How long?" he asked.

She tilted her head to the side. "Pardon?"

"How long before your clothing is dry?"

"An hour or two I should think."

One hundred and twenty minutes of gazing on her, of having her within reach. He was residing in both heaven and hell. The whiskey was having a lethargic effect on him because suddenly he was grateful she'd taken a dip into the water, was here with him now. He settled back to enjoy her company. "So I shared with you earlier. Now it's your turn to share with me."

Her eyes widened slightly. "Oh, right. The most intimate thing I've done or imagined doing with a man."

He lifted his glass in a salute. "You don't have to tell me who he is or who you imagined him being."

"Oh, I wouldn't. You wouldn't tell me who your lady love was so I won't give you any names either."

Lady love. Strange how he'd never really pondered Lady M in those terms, even though at the time he'd considered himself wrapped up in her spell. Also strange was that he didn't contemplate reading poetry or sonnets to Gina. He enjoyed conversing with her far too much to consider giving up a single conversation in order to recite another's words to her. "Yet you will provide details."

She nodded, sipped her brandy. "Although to be honest, it's not really something I imagined before I spoke with Venus, and since then I've not been able to get it out of my mind."

His fingers tightened on his glass. "What exactly did she say?" The words came out harsher than he'd intended.

She laughed, a tinkling of bells, chimes, and crystal being flicked. "I think it bothers you that I spent time with her."

"Bothered is not exactly the right word." It was the perfect word. "I'm simply intrigued to know what she might have told you, to view the act from a lady's perspective."

She shifted. The knee disappeared, reappeared. "We didn't get to discuss a great deal because we were interrupted—"

She gave him a pointed look. He refused to take the bait and blush. "—but she was describing how a woman can experience pleasure without losing her virginity." She looked into the fire. "She told me men like to touch everywhere, that some use their tongues in wicked ways. She was on the verge of explaining exactly how it all transpires when you barged in." Her gaze came back to land on him. Hard. For some strange reason, his cock twitched. "I was quite put out with you. So perhaps you should give me some consideration and explain precisely what she didn't get a chance to."

"I'll do you one better. I'll show you."

She should have been scandalized by his offer. Instead, as he stood, she looked at the large bare hand he was holding out to her, and the only thought she seemed capable of forming was that he'd be touching her with that hand, that he would stroke and caress. That he might do a good deal more than that.

After taking a deep breath, she placed her hand in his, fought to breathe as his fingers closed firmly around hers. No hesitation on his part, no doubts.

"If at any time you change your mind, you have but to say and we'll stop." He drew her nearer until only a hairsbreadth separated them. With his free hand, he flicked the blanket off one of her shoulders and it fell to the floor, leaving a good bit of her legs exposed. "My shirt looks much better on you than it does on me."

"I would disagree. It's too large."

His gaze dipped to her nude calves. "There is that."

Her toes squirmed, and it was all she could do not to let the squirming travel upward. She was going to be bold and daring tonight, not at all dull.

Unexpectedly, he lifted her into his arms. With a squeak, she wrapped her arms around his neck. "We're not going to stay in here?"

"A bed would serve us better."

She nodded, and he began striding from the room. "I assume we won't sit cross-legged on it and talk."

"There may be some talking. Legs might get crossed." He winked at her. "But it will be far different from what you experienced the other night."

She ran a hand along his jaw. It was bristly and prickly. She liked the feel of it, the texture, the roughness. Before the night was done, it might abrade her skin. She was anticipating it with a headiness that made her realize she was somewhat wanton.

Up the stairs he went. She felt delicate and precious in his arms. While she knew it was wrong, might result in her downfall, she couldn't seem to care.

At the landing, he turned down a short hallway and into a room with a massive four-poster bed. Not the room where she had bathed and changed. These were his chambers; she knew it without being told. It smelled of him. It reminded her of him.

While he was fair, the furniture was dark, spoke to a part of him that called to the darker elements: vices, addictions, wickedness. Yet there was hope here in the pastel green of the wallpaper, the forest green of the duvet.

He lowered her feet to the thick rug beside the bed, cradled her face between his palms. "We're going to get very intimate, Gina, but I need you to know that I won't dishonor you by taking your virginity."

She wanted to tell him that he would only honor her if he did, but as though knowing she would object, he pressed his thumbs to her lips. "But when we are done here, you will have been well and truly pleasured."

"What of you?"

He lowered his head. "I believe I will never know any greater satisfaction." His lips met hers, and she tasted the whiskey he'd sipped earlier. Opening her mouth to him, she found herself drowning in the sensations of rich flavors, sharp fragrances, the heat of his skin, the roughness of his jaw. She scraped her nails up into his hair, loving the way the curls tangled themselves around her fingers. Groaning low, he pressed her flush against him, until her breasts were flattened against his chest.

He dragged his mouth along the underside of her chin and desire sluiced through her. After nibbling at the sensitive skin below her ear, he soothed it with little laps of his tongue. "I've wanted to do that for so long," he rasped.

"I've wanted you to. And I've yearned to do this." Leaning in, rising up on her toes, she pressed her mouth to his throat, where the buttons he'd left undone revealed a narrow V of skin. He was salty on her tongue. His low growl sent shivers of pleasure coursing through her. It excited her to know she could elicit such a reaction from him, that he wasn't immune to her touch.

Drawing back, he placed his hands on her shoulders and turned her around. She felt a slight tug on her hair, realized he was unbraiding the strands she'd so meticulously woven together following her bath. When all the locks were free, he plowed his hands into her hair, massaged her scalp. With a sigh, she closed her eyes.

"So glorious," he rasped. "Goes all the way down to your bum."

"Gentlemen do not discuss that part of a woman's anatomy."

"You're about to discover I'm no gentleman."

She was very much looking forward to that.

Gathering up all the tresses, he draped them over her right shoulder. "Set the first button that is secured free," he ordered. "But only the one."

If he asked, she'd loosen them all. What a scandalous thought. She did as he instructed, and once her hands fell to her sides, he eased the opening of his shirt aside until it was almost off her shoulders. His open mouth landed against the nape of her neck, bringing with it heat and moisture. She couldn't hold back her soft moan as he journeyed over her skin, along her spine. His hands closed around her arms as though he would hold her in place. Only she wasn't going anywhere, except possibly to twist about and take possession of the luscious mouth that was doing such deliciously tantalizing things.

"Did you ever go to that room at the brothel where people could watch you?" she asked.

"No. What transpires between a lady and me is private, only for the two of us. I never discuss my encounters. You're safe with me tonight, Gina. No one will ever learn that I know all the wickedly wonderful little sounds you make when lost in rapture."

"And if I don't become lost?"

"Oh, you will, sweetheart."

And she couldn't help but wonder if in becoming lost she might also become found.

CHAPTER 9

He'd never been intimate with a woman of such purity, one who was experiencing all the many different facets of pleasure for the first time. It inflamed his own yearnings to know she was not merely a virgin at her core, but that her entire body was an untouched temple that had never been explored by any man. He was humbled by the gift she had presented him.

He trailed his mouth to the sensitive spot behind her ear. "You're to tell me if I do anything you don't like."

"And if I do like what you're doing?" she asked on a soft sigh.

"Tell me that as well—with words, with sighs, moans, a bit of squirming."

"You're going to make me squirm?"

"That's my goal. Don't hold back, Gina. I will not sit in judgment of your reactions."

He guided his lips and tongue along the silken path just above where the collar of his shirt rested. "Another button," he ordered.

She obeyed and he eased his shirt off her shoulder. It shouldn't have hit him like a punch to the gut. It wasn't as though he hadn't seen it before when she wore a ball gown. He didn't know if he'd ever found anything as sensual, however, as her in his clothing. Memories of her were sure to flood his mind anytime he wore the shirt in the future, and he suspected it would quickly become thin and frayed with its constant use.

He took his mouth on a leisurely journey over her shoulder. She sighed, a long drawn out, almost painful sound but he knew it wasn't pain she was feeling. "Another."

He slipped his finger beneath the cloth at her other shoulder and slid the linen down. "All of them."

His voice sounded as though he were strangling. He was aware of the little tugs on his shirt. She didn't hesitate. She trusted him. Wholly. Completely. Absolutely. He should command her to button herself up to her throat. He should spin on his heel and march from the room in long strides that would quickly get him beyond reach of her.

Instead he stood there and kept his mouth shut. When her hands fell to her sides, he lowered the cloth, not even bothering to watch it drift to the floor, too mesmerized by the perfection unveiled.

"My God, but you are beautiful."

The reverence in his voice brought tears to her eyes. Tillie, Tillie was the beautiful one, the one who'd swept into London and brought lords to their knees. Gina's uncle had been forced to make a deal with Rexton in order for Gina to draw anyone's attention. She'd wanted dukes and earls to fight over her, marquesses and viscounts to vie for her affection. She'd wanted her dance cards filled, the soles of her dancing slippers worn thin, and her pick of proposals.

Now all she wanted was for Andrew Mabry to touch her.

Oh, she was a wicked girl, and she didn't care.

Slowly, so slowly, she turned around. The man looked to be in torment as his gaze dipped and lifted back to her face. Without prompting, she reached for his buttons.

"Gina—"

"I want to see you, too," she admitted, before her courage left her.

He remained still until all the buttons she could reach were loose, then he pulled his shirttails from his trousers, dragged his shirt over his head, and tossed it aside. Lacking his discipline, she flattened her palms against his chest, smiled. "You're beautiful, too."

She raised her gaze to his. "I want to see all of you."

"It's only fair I suppose."

He unfastened his trousers, lowered them, straightened. Her mouth went dry as she stared at his proudly jutting member. "You have a magnificent cock."

Laughing, he picked her up, tossed her onto the bed, and joined her there, stretched out along her side, raised up on an elbow. His eyes on hers, he trailed his finger along her chin. "Did Venus tell you to say that?"

"She said some were magnificent. Yours is much nicer than the other one I saw. Can I touch it?"

"Ah, Christ." He pressed his forehead to hers, nodded.

Reaching down, she wrapped her fingers around the hot, hard shaft. Covering her hand with his, he guided it up and down. "I like the way it feels," she whispered.

"Oh, I like the way it feels, too. Explore all you wish."

They explored each other, touching, caressing, stroking. She squeezed his buttocks, scraped her fingers up his side.

He cradled her breast, kneading it gently, flicking his tongue over her nipple until it peaked, then lowering his mouth to it. She might have been embarrassed by her moan if he hadn't groaned. He shifted until he was nestled between her thighs, his stomach pressed against the most intimate part of her.

"I can't reach you," she bemoaned.

"Preservation, sweetheart." He kissed the inside of her breast, the underside. "I was on the verge of going mad . . . and embarrassing myself."

"Venus said sometimes she touches a man and he spills his seed right then and there. Is that what you mean by embarrassing yourself?"

"Mmm." He licked his way down her ribs. "But tonight is about pleasuring you."

"I want us both pleasured."

"You first." He nipped at her hip. It tickled more than hurt.

"For that to happen, I need your cock, though, don't I?"

He gave her a deliciously wicked and sensual smile. "I have a very talented tongue."

He slid down farther, blew on her curls. She couldn't believe his face was right there, between her thighs. Raising her knees, she placed her soles on his back, tangled her fingers in his hair. With the tip of his finger, he parted her most intimate lips. "You are so wet."

She couldn't help it. She laughed.

"You find that funny?"

"Somerdale said I was as sweet as sugar and would melt if I got wet."

"Oh, you're going to melt ... into a pool of burning desire." He lowered his mouth and proceeded to demonstrate that he did indeed have a most clever tongue.

Of their own accord, her hips tilted up, offering her very essence to him. He feasted, sending sensation after sensation roiling through her. She'd never felt anything so sublime. Venus hadn't told her about this, hadn't told her that pleasure was a whirlwind of escalating awareness. Throughout her body, nerve endings tingled—even areas to which he wasn't giving his utmost attention. Oh, but those that he was ...

She couldn't hold back the sighs and moans. Her head pressed back into the pillow, even as she wanted to curl forward. The intimacy he demonstrated nearly caused her to come undone. She couldn't imagine allowing any other man to lick and suckle there. Him, all she wanted was him, doing things he shouldn't.

She loved that about him, that he taught her the wickedest things, didn't consider her too innocent or proper to know what transpired between men and women. That he brought her close to a peak, nearly brought her out of her mind.

Her entire body wanted to clamp around him, hold him close, prevent him from taking her further into the realm of pleasure. The escalating tide frightened her. It was unlike anything she'd ever experienced, but if she was going to make this journey toward ultimate fulfillment, she wanted to make it with him.

She felt as though she'd been cast adrift on an ocean tide, ebbing and flowing, then she was riding the crest, crying out as her back arched, she held him close with her fingers, her thighs, any part of her that could reach him, touch him.

He stilled. Breathing heavily, she collapsed onto the bed, stared at the canopy, striving to regain some semblance of control.

He kissed the inside of one thigh, then the other. Glancing down, she captured and held his gaze. "I want you inside me."

Easing up, he left a trail of kisses in his wake until he was looking down on her. "No. I won't ruin you, Gina."

Desperately, she cradled his face between her hands. "It's not fair for you to witness me coming completely undone. I want—need—to know you are as affected."

He lowered his mouth to the underside of her jaw. "I'll give you a bit, just a bit."

Shifting, he began rubbing his cock over her little, but extremely sensitive, bud. She reveled in the hardness and his heat reigniting her, his groan. The wonder of it, the closeness, the intimacy. He repositioned himself, and she was aware of the head of his cock poised against her opening. It wasn't enough.

She wiggled.

"Don't." The word came out terse. "I only want to feel you for a moment." More gently, more sweetly.

"I'm a terrible wanton. I won't object if you go further."

"Your husband will."

She squeezed her eyes shut at the reminder, the affirmation, that he wouldn't marry her. If forced to give a name to their relationship, she couldn't. More than friends, not quite lovers. Later she would mourn what couldn't be between them, but not now. Opening her eyes, she dragged her fingers up and down his back, felt the tenseness in his firm muscles. Working her hand between their bodies, she wrapped her fingers around him and began to stroke the length of him.

His groan echoing pure torment made her giddy. Burying his face against her neck, he wrapped his arms around her, held her close. His breaths quickened, his moans increased. With a low growl, he jerked away from her opening, and hot fluids coated her palm.

He went still, so still. With her free hand, she scraped her fingers along his scalp and held him in the curve of her shoulder, wondering if she'd ever again know such contentment.

It was inconceivable to him that he could know such satisfaction without a complete taking of her. But he did.

He'd loved watching her climax. When she'd asked for more from him, how could he not give it?

Already hovering on the precipice, he'd known it wouldn't take much. The hardest thing he'd ever done was not to push forward and bury himself to the hilt in that lovely wet and heated notch. He suspected one thrust would have had his seed pouring forth. But he would not dishonor her, would not do anything to lessen her chances of marriage with a titled gentleman.

"As much as I am loath to leave this bed, we must get you back into my parents' residence."

"I know. Andrew—"

He touched his finger to her lips when he desperately wanted to put his mouth there. "It's best if we not say anything more. Tonight's adventure needs to come to a close."

She nodded. "I shall never forget it."

His worry was that he wouldn't either, or worse: she had spoiled him for anyone else.

Within the confines of the carriage, Gina snuggled against Andrew's side, with his arm securely around her shoulders. If their journey never ended, if they never reached his parents' residence, she would be forever content.

He'd assisted her in putting on her clothing—even though it was still damp. He'd brushed and braided her hair. Because there had been no vanity in the room, she'd been unable to study his reflection in a mirror as he administered to her needs while she sat on the bed, but she knew she'd always remember the gentleness with which he'd tidied the strands. He made her feel treasured, protected, loved.

Which was silly. He didn't love her. She didn't delude herself into thinking he did. She was a bit of fun for the night. He was always game for fun.

It was in his nature. She'd taken advantage, but she didn't regret it.

"Is it different with every woman?" she asked softly.

He drew her in closer against his side. "The mechanics are very much the same, but the details—her fragrance, the silkiness of her skin, the small sounds she makes—differ."

"So you'll have memories that are unique to me, to no one else."

His mouth pressed to the top of her head. "You will always stand apart, Gina."

"Is it difficult to be with someone else . . . after you've been with someone?"

"If you're thinking of the man you'll marry—you'll love him, you'll want to be with him, you'll desire an even greater intimacy than what we shared—and everything about me will fade away."

She very much doubted that.

"As it should," he said quietly, his tone reflecting regret and sorrow.

"I doubt I'll forget my first."

"It was only a partial first."

Still she'd never before known such pleasure, passion, or desire.

The carriage came to a halt, but he didn't immediately release his hold on her. She took some comfort in that, that the parting was as difficult for him as it was for her.

When the door opened, he slowly extricated himself from around her, stepped out, then handed her down. He didn't release his hold on her hand, but held firm as they walked up the steps. Once they reached the door, he didn't hesitate to take her in his arms and kiss her.

Deeply, thoroughly, hungrily, as though he were a man being offered his last meal.

She didn't want to contemplate that she would never again feel his lips on hers, his tongue sliding over hers. Instead she focused on every nuance, on committing them all to memory. He would not fade, time spent with him would never fade. Eventually she would have to close her heart off to him in order to open it up to someone else. Determined not to live her life without love, she would find a way to carry on, to survive without a man who stirred so many incredible sensations and frightening emotions within her.

He brought her so much joy and happiness, but in the end he would break her heart, because he could not—would not—love her. Because he wanted a life without entanglements and responsibilities. He was someone with whom she could have fun and excitement but not a future. She was going to be grateful for the minutes she had with him and not mourn the time she didn't.

Drawing back, he held her gaze, stroked his fingers over her cheek. "You deserve a man who can love you with all his heart."

And he couldn't, thanks to one stupid, obnoxious woman she didn't even know. "I hope someday you will learn to love again. You deserve to be happy."

He grinned. "I am happy."

He unlocked the door, opened it, peered inside. "All is quiet." Stepping back, he placed a final kiss on her forehead. "Good night, Gina. Enjoy the Waverly ball this evening."

She almost told him she'd skip it if he wanted to enjoy

another adventure with her, but the Season was nearing its end and if she didn't want to be on the marriage block next year, she needed to attend every social engagement to which she was invited. "I'm rather certain I will. Your sister is chaperoning me, and will provide me with an introduction to any lord I haven't already met. Not that there are many anymore. Which is quite a relief. For a time there, I feared the fault for the gents' lack of interest rested more with me rather than Tillie's scandal."

"You could never be at fault."

"Scandal has such dire consequences."

"Which is the very reason you need to pop inside before we're spotted."

He was correct, even though she wanted to stay out here with him until the lark sang. "Good night, Andrew." Rising up on her toes, she brushed a quick kiss across his bristled chin before dashing into the residence.

He closed the door, and she hurried up the stairs to her room. Each adventure with him was better than the last. It saddened her to know they'd soon be coming to an end.

CHAPTER 10

It was an odd thing, the following evening, to dance with an assortment of gentlemen at the Waverly ball, while maintaining the appearance of innocence. Gina was rather stupefied that none noticed she'd recently been consumed by passion. Pleasure was still radiating from her, her skin was sensitive to the touch, her limbs were at once lethargic and energized.

While she'd managed to slip into the residence without anyone the wiser, she rather wished she had been caught, but Andrew would resent her for that, would resent her forcing him into marriage. He loved having the life of a bachelor. She couldn't live with herself if she stole that away from him.

So her only recourse for marriage involved welcoming the attentiveness of one of the gentlemen who now approached her with such ease. She might have favored them more had they, like Somerdale, sought her out while she lived beneath the shroud of scandal. While the earl's devotion had been relatively subtle, at least he'd not shied completely away from her. However, if he ever learned of her recent scandalous behavior, he'd no doubt scamper for the hills. Not that she'd blame him.

Although she did think it unfair that men could seek out pleasure before marriage and women couldn't. It had been so lovely she nearly burst into song whenever she thought about it—which was far too often. Fortunately, the gents thought it was their skill at dancing that caused her bright smile.

Lord Benson was her present partner. He was exceedingly graceful but not nearly as graceful at Andrew. She rather wished he was here tonight, not only to share a dance but the entirety of the evening. She missed him, and while she knew it wasn't wise, she couldn't seem to help herself.

"I preferred your earlier smile to your present frown," Lord Benson said.

Heat warmed her face. "My apologies. My mind drifted off to where it shouldn't."

"That does not bode well for my courtship."

Was he courting her? He'd yet to call on her, but he had sent flowers.

"I realize I have not been that attentive, but when your sister returns, I intend to call upon you—if you have no objections."

"None whatsoever. It would be lovely."

"When does she return?"

"Not for a few more days, although you are welcome to call on me at the Greystone residence."

He grinned. "I shall do so."

The music wafted into silence, and he escorted her from the dance floor to an area where several ladies were sitting.

"I shall count the minutes until I can call on you on the morrow," Lord Benson said, taking her hand and pressing a kiss to her gloved knuckles.

"I look forward to it."

With a quick bow, he strode away.

"You know he'll be taxing his brain to count that high," a deep, masculine voice said from behind her, the richness of it shimmering up her spine.

Gina swung around. Her heart hammered within her chest. Andrew stood there in his black swallow-tailed coat, pristine white shirt, and cravat. "That was rather unkind."

"He would make you miserable."

She didn't want to discuss Lord Benson or his suitability. "I didn't think you were coming."

"I changed my mind."

"I do wish I'd known. I'd have saved a dance for you. As it is, my card is full."

"When is your waltz with Lord Manville?"

Although she had told him at the Twin Dragons that Manville had claimed a dance, she hadn't specified it would be a waltz. She wasn't going to give him the satisfaction of asking how he knew the particulars, although secretly she was rather pleased he'd gone to the trouble to find out. "Next actually. I must find him."

"He's in the card room where he was foolish enough to wager away his waltz with you."

It was ridiculous how giddy his words made her because she suspected she knew the answer to the question she was on the verge of asking. "To whom did he lose the wager?"

"Me." He held out his gloved hand.

She placed her hand in his. "I do hope you didn't cheat."

His fingers closing around hers, he gave her a sultry grin. "You'd be disappointed if I didn't."

She would have been. Shame on her.

Just as the orchestra started the next tune, he led her onto the dance floor. Once she was secure in his arms, gliding over the polished wood, she asked, "Did you really cheat?"

"I always cheat when the wager involves something I don't wish to lose."

"You wanted to dance with me."

"It's the only reason I'm here."

"I wasn't certain we'd have any more adventures."

"One small one—in a room filled with people—can't hurt. Besides I wanted to ensure you were all right." His gaze held hers, intently searching, as though he sought to uncover all the secrets held in her heart and soul. "Last night shouldn't have happened. I feared this morning you might have awoken with regrets."

Difficult to awaken when she hadn't slept. "No regrets. Although you could have called on me to get your answers."

"My parents are turning out to be terrible chaperones. I believe I mentioned earlier the safety of a room filled with people."

Glancing around, keeping her voice low, she dared to ask, "Do you have regrets?"

"Nary a one. But I'm not the one seeking marriage."

No, he wasn't, while she was. "Do you know what I find most fascinating? Outwardly nothing about me changed. No one looking at me seems to have a clue regarding the naughty things I've done."

"And inwardly?"

His eyes held concern. She wanted to see him smile, hear him laugh. "There are some changes. How could there not be? A person can't unknow what she knows. I look at my suitors tonight, at each dance partner, and imagine far more intimate encounters."

His fingers jerked around hers, tightened. His brow furrowed. "What exactly do you imagine?"

"Different things."

"Do they please you?"

"Well, I'm certainly not going to imagine something that wouldn't please me." She chuckled. "Don't look so disgruntled. None can compare to you."

He shook his head, relaxed his face. "But I want them to. For you, I want them to be better than me."

"I don't know that there's better or worse. I suspect there will just be *different*."

"Words of wisdom from Venus, I assume."

She smiled. "She might have mentioned something along those lines. I've had a most educational few nights since Tillie's departure. They shall stand me in good stead."

Finally, he gave her a devilish grin. "I'm sure they will."

They spoke no more as he swept her into the fray. She wished all her remaining dances belonged to him. She loved the way he held her, the way he watched her, the way they moved in tandem. She suspected once she was married, he'd never dance with her again. Oh, their paths would cross during family gatherings. They would be polite, cordial, but there would be no heated glances, no passions stirring beneath the surface.

The music ended long before she was ready. "Would you like to look my dance card over to determine if there is someone else you can bilk out of a dance?"

Slowly he shook his head. "No, I suspect we've already set enough tongues to wagging." Never taking his gaze from hers, he brought her hand to his lips, allowed the heat from his mouth to seep through the cloth. "Enjoy the remainder of your evening, Miss Hammersley."

Watching him stride away, she wondered if there would ever come a time when she didn't feel a small measure of pain when he left her behind.

He shouldn't have come. He shouldn't have danced with her. Yet, where she was concerned, he seemed unable to stop himself from doing the things he ought not.

A few minutes earlier, he'd seen Somerdale escort her into the gardens, and everything within him screamed that he should follow, that he should interfere, that he should ensure nothing untoward happened.

He'd made it to the edge of the terrace before rational thought returned. It was not his place to stop a gentleman from wooing her. He couldn't be that selfish. So he moved to the distant shadows and listened as the breeze stirred the leaves, waited, like a forlorn pup that knew his mistress might never return to him. If she was smart, she wouldn't. And if he knew anything at all about Gina, it was that she was smart.

"Hello, Lord Andrew."

A voice that had once shimmered through him and brought pleasure now failed to stir even the slightest interest. Still, he knew it was dangerous not to face the Countess of Montley, and so he did. "Lady M."

"You used to address me with such cherished endearments."

"I cared for you then. I don't now."

"Oh, come. I'm certain there is still a part of you that stirs for me."

Not even a quarter of an inch. Once he'd been mad for her. He'd thought it was love. Only now did he realize it hadn't come close. What he'd felt for her had been a wild infatuation, but it would have eventually burned out. He might not have had the good fortune to realize it until after he'd wed her—if he'd had the chance to do so. But her own marriage had prevented that grave error in judgment from occurring. Strange how what had once pained him now filled him with overwhelming relief.

Stepping forward, she flattened her palm above his beating heart. It didn't change its tempo. He would have given a stronger reaction if a fly had landed on him.

"I've missed you," she said, her tone filled with innuendo and promises.

Had he missed her? In the beginning perhaps, but he hadn't thought about her in intimate terms in years. Unlike Gina, whom he knew he would think about every day until he died. He would think of her smile and her laughter. He would remember her sitting on a bed with a harlot, grinning as she bested him at cards. He would think of her whenever he smelled violets, heard the shuffle of cards, tasted brandy, looked into green eyes.

"Do you recall how we used to meet at the Nightingale?" she asked, filling the silence that was stretching between them. "What fun we had. I was thinking perhaps it's time we had a little reunion."

She began to slide her hand lower; he wrapped his fingers around her wrist, stilling her actions. "I'm no longer interested in what you have to offer."

She tilted up her chin. "Is it that silly little American heiress? I saw you waltzing with her, saw the way you looked at her . . . the way you once looked at me."

"I never looked at you the way I look at her." He didn't say the words to hurt her, but rather because they were true, because Gina deserved to have them spoken aloud, was worthy of his making it clear that what he felt for her in no way resembled what he'd once felt for Lady M. When he gazed on Gina, he saw dreams, possibilities, adventures between the sheets and beyond them.

With Lady M, he'd only ever seen sex. He couldn't recall a single conversation with her of any significance. With her it had always been just ribald talk, innuendo, and crudity. She'd inflamed his desires, but they were quickly doused.

With Gina, the passion always persisted, never dimmed. He suspected it never would.

"She possesses a fortune," Lady M said. "You can't possibly think she'll settle for a spare when she could have a titled gentleman."

No, she wouldn't settle nor would he want her to. Her happiness was more important than his. He wanted her to have everything she'd ever hoped to hold. Willingly he would stand in the shadows and find contentment in watching the joy she would exhibit in realizing her dreams with someone other than him.

His silence must have unnerved Lady M because she jerked her wrist free of his hold and spit out, "You're a fool, Andrew. You always were."

No. Before he'd been an idiot. There was a difference. While he may have foolishly fallen for Gina, he couldn't regret it when she made him more than he'd ever been.

S omerdale had claimed two dances in a row, but rather than taking her onto the dance floor for the first one, he'd invited her to take a stroll through the garden with him. She'd actually welcomed the opportunity to step out into the night and have the cooler air brushing over her skin.

Ever since her dance with Andrew, she'd been far too warm, constantly reliving much of the evening before. Every touch and caress. Every lap of his tongue. The feel of him covering her, the way his muscles knotted and bunched. His growls and groans. The smoldering heat in his eyes—

". . . your uncle or Rexton?"

The tail end of Somerdale's question intruded on her musings. "Pardon?"

He chuckled low, self-consciously. "How much did you not hear?"

"I fear quite a bit. My apologies. I was lost in the beauty of the gardens." Even though they were ensconced in darkness.

"I was saying that I don't think it should come as any surprise to you that I am quite taken with you and think we are well suited."

Oh dear God. Surely this was not going where she suspected it might be.

"I wasn't certain with whom I should speak regarding my intentions: your uncle or Rexton."

Her uncle was family, blood. He resided in London, was terribly convenient. Rexton, her new brother-by-marriage, was still at Kingsbrook Park enjoying his new bride. Terribly inconvenient that. "Rexton, I should think since Tillie is the one who has always been more responsible for me than Uncle, who merely provided me with an escort to balls when Tillie was not welcomed."

As he nodded, he didn't appear too happy, which should have pleased her no end—to know he was anxious to move their relationship forward, to possibly ask for her hand in marriage. Instead she feared all her adventures, all the excitement, all the exhilaration would be stolen from her life. Her time with Andrew would come to an abrupt end.

She wanted one more night with him, one more spectacular night with enough naughtiness to last a lifetime. And she wasn't above using blackmail to get it.

But when they returned to the ballroom, she couldn't find Andrew. He wasn't on the dance floor or at its edge. Neither was he in the card room, the smoking room, or the refreshments room. Apparently he'd left.

By the time the ball ended, it would be too late to seek him out tonight. But she was rather certain she knew how to go about seeing him on the morrow.

CHAPTER 11

The Nightingale tonight at 10.
   —G

"**W**hat the bloody hell is this?" Andrew whispered harshly, waving the missive he'd received in the late afternoon at Gina. He'd arrived at his parents' residence five minutes earlier, supposedly to enjoy dinner, when in fact he'd needed to confront her with what he was certain was a fairly mad scheme.

"Do you not read?" she asked innocently, standing in the center of the parlor while they waited to be joined by his parents. Did she have to look so incredibly enticing? Did she not have any rags to wear?

"Bloody hell, of course I read." *Bloody hell* had been the litany rushing through his mind ever since he'd read her words. He'd made a grave error in judgment allowing the other night to happen, because he couldn't stop thinking about it, couldn't stop wanting another night with her, and then her bloody note had arrived.

"Then it should be fairly obvious."

"You can't go to the Nightingale Club. It's unseemly. Besides if I didn't ruin you before, I'm certainly not going to do it there."

"I'm not asking you to. I simply want to see it."

"No."

"Hmm." With incredible elegance, she glided over to the fireplace, stroked her finger over the mantel and his gut clenched with the reminder of how she'd stroked him. "I wonder what your brother is going to say when he learns you took me to a brothel."

"He's not going to learn because you swore to keep our outing a secret. I shall be terribly disappointed to learn you're a lying tart."

Another stroke of the marble. What the devil was wrong with him that he should find it so provocative? All morning he'd been reliving every touch she'd bestowed on him. The night they'd gone rowing he'd known her excuse of not wanting to return here drenched had been ridiculous, but he'd gladly accepted it as a viable reason not to rush her home because he'd not yet been willing to give up his time with her.

"Better a lying tart than a boring one."

"Gina—"

She faced him, clasping her hands together. "I think he's on the verge of asking your brother for my hand in marriage."

Her words jumbled in his brain, made no sense. "What are you talking about?"

"Somerdale. When we were walking in the gardens last night, he asked to whom he should speak regarding his intentions toward me."

There was a sudden roaring between his ears that made it difficult to think. "Do you want to marry him?"

"I like him well enough and I think we're well suited."

"He's gambled away a good bit of his inheritance."

She shrugged. "And mine will fill his coffers. It's the reason gentlemen prefer heiresses, isn't it?"

You are deserving of a man who would marry you if you were a pauper.

She took a step toward him. "I suspect things are going to move rather quickly once Tillie and Rexton return. I want one more night of adventure. Something wicked and scandalous." Another step forward. Tilting back her head, she met and held his gaze.

"I want one more night with you doing something I shouldn't, something I can look back on with fond memories, that will make me smile. A night when I wasn't dull . . . before I settle into a life of porridge every morning."

As he sat in the parlor of the Nightingale Club, he called himself every sort of fool. He'd given in to her desires and brought her here when no good could come of it.

They'd arrived in a hansom. Beneath her cloak, Gina

had been clutching a domino mask, which led him to believe she'd have come here without him if he hadn't reluctantly agreed to bring her—if she'd been able to find the locale. Knowing her as he did, he was fairly certain she'd have sniffed it out one way or another. Better to come here under his protection than alone. Or so he'd argued with himself.

He hadn't visited the infamous residence since he'd ended his affair with Lady M all those years back. While initially he'd had fond memories of the place, they'd been soured by the countess's revelations regarding her marital status. It was still difficult to believe he'd been such an idiot. Thank God, he no longer thought with the lower half of his body.

Then what the deuce are you doing here now?

Gina was going to want to go up those stairs and into one of those bedchambers. She wasn't going to be content to have a glance around the parlor, note the various flirtations, and identify which lords were about.

When they'd arrived, he'd escorted her to a back door where the ladies entered. Someone would assist her in disrobing and putting on silk that clung to the skin and flowed with her movements. Then she would be escorted here, and he would claim her so fast it would make the other gents dizzy. The mask would conceal her identity—

Only it didn't. He realized that the moment she strolled over the threshold. How could any man watch the vision in pink gliding into the room and not recognize her? How could they see the shining blond hair draped over one shoulder and not envision it tucked up into an elaborate coiffure at a ball?

How could they not estimate her height, take in the luscious dips and swells outlined by silk and not know they were looking at Gina Hammersley?

This had been a terrible, awful idea. He didn't recall shoving himself out of the chair but suddenly he was standing in front of her. The mask covered three quarters of her face, leaving only her mouth and chin visible, but how could any man who had danced with her not spend his time memorizing the perfect bow shape of her upper lip, not envisioned himself nibbling on the full lower lip? How could they not recognize the dark pink that begged a man to taste them?

How could any man look into her eyes and not know that no other woman in England had eyes so green, so fetching, so tempting?

He was in trouble because there was nothing he wanted more than to take her up those stairs and possess her completely, to claim her as his own, to make those eyes darken with desire, to make those lips part in wonder, to hear her sighs and moans ringing in his ears.

She smiled, and he was lost. His resolve to honor her, to not take from her what could never be returned, cracked and buckled under the weight of how desperately he wanted her.

"Lord Andrew Mabry, you despicable blackguard! I knew it was you!"

It took Andrew a moment to break free of the spell she'd placed over him. Looking past her, he saw the Earl of Montley standing there. Good Lord, he was wielding a pistol. The room had gone completely quiet and still.

"Montley—"

"Come here, you unfaithful wench," the man barked, and Andrew realized the earl thought Gina was his wife.

Stepping in front of Gina, Andrew tried to push her even farther back, not at all happy with the resistance she was emitting. "She's not your wife, man."

"Don't be absurd. Do you think I don't recognize my own countess?"

"Apparently you don't."

"Come here, wife, or I shall shoot off his cock!"

Gina stepped forward. Andrew wrapped his fingers around her arm. She flung him off. "My lord, I am not your wife."

"You deceitful liar!" He aimed the pistol at Andrew, low, very low, cocked it—

Then Gina did the very worst thing she could have done.

She flung off her mask.

Lord Montley stared agape.

It was all the evidence she required that the man was flummoxed. Darting forward—

"Gina!" Andrew snaked his arm around her waist and drew her back just as she snatched the gun from the earl's grasp.

"I'm fine," she told him as she put the hammer back into place and expertly removed the bullets. She did wish he hadn't used her name, although based on the open mouths, wide eyes, and the whispers of "Miss Hammersley?" from the onlookers, her identity was no longer a secret.

She was aware of blurred movement as Andrew lunged past her. The sound of bone cracking rent the air. Montley hit the floor.

Andrew had struck him. It was unconscionable, the satisfaction that whipped through her.

Legs akimbo, Andrew stood over the fallen lord. "I've not been with your wife in years. With your theatrics, you have caused an innocent woman to put her reputation at risk, you toad."

"My wife is here somewhere. I know she is. I followed her. I will find her."

"She's not worth it while the woman you threatened is worth everything." He turned to face Gina, gave her a sardonic grin. "Enough adventure for you?"

"**W**hat happened tonight will be all over London by morning, the key players identified by name, your reputation ruined. No one will believe you were there out of mere curiosity."

As the hansom traveled through the streets at a rapid clip, she heard defeat in Andrew's voice. "I suppose we should have made use of a room then. If my reputation is to be tarnished, we should have taken advantage of it."

"Gina, this isn't funny. We can't make light of it. It isn't going to go away."

She knew that. "Lady Montley, was she that woman from all those years ago? The one you loved? The one you didn't know was married?"

"Gina—"

"Was she?"

"Yes. It appears she's up to her old tricks. I suppose she's never been faithful to him."

She couldn't care less about the woman's promiscuity. What bothered her was that the earl had thought Gina was his wife. She couldn't recall ever meeting the woman. A sick, roiling feeling kept her stomach churning, doubts kept her mind reeling. "Do I remind you of her?" *Is that the reason you've given me attention, taken me to your bed?*

"Good God, no. Why would you think that?" He sounded truly horrified.

"Montley mistook me for his wife."

"The man is out of his mind with jealousy and rage. He wasn't thinking clearly."

"Is her hair blond?"

He sighed. "Yes, but not as fair as yours."

The room had been dimly lit so obviously the earl had not been able to detect the slight difference. "We must be of the same height and body shape."

"Gina." He twisted around until he was facing her more squarely, or as squarely as possible when they sat beside each other in the cramped conveyance. "She's taller than you. She hasn't your delicate bone structure."

He cradled her face. "Her eyes . . ." His head tilted slightly. "They don't sparkle the way yours do." He stroked his thumb over her mouth. "I can't remember how she tasted or how she felt in my arms."

His scoff, low and self-deprecating, echoed around them.

"Once I thought I would never forget anything about her. Now I can hardly remember anything at all. But I do know that I would never mistake another woman—not even your twin should you have one—for you."

His words were spoken with such sincerity that she nearly wept. "We're going to be in a great deal of trouble, aren't we?"

"Unfortunately, I fear I've mucked things up rather badly for you." He wrapped his arm around her shoulders, drew her in close. "But we shall weather it."

She was grateful for his confidence, although she didn't share it. Having watched Tillie survive her scandal, Gina wasn't certain she'd be able to survive her own.

CHAPTER 12

"What the bloody hell were you thinking?"

Andrew didn't flinch at his brother's harsh words, shouted at him, within their father's library. He deserved the anger, the disappointment. He deserved it and a good deal more.

A servant had been sent to Kingsbrook Park to fetch the Marquess and Marchioness of Rexton. It had taken hours. Andrew had been made to wait between the dark walls and musty books, with his father staring at him in stony silence. His mother had stayed with Gina in her room until her sister arrived. Then the duchess had joined them here, saying not a word, merely lowering herself gracefully into a chair, her gaze riveted on him where he stood near the fireplace.

"Andrew, I'm speaking to you," Rex stated harshly.

"No, you're yelling. And I should think the answer is obvious: I wasn't thinking."

"I warned you to stay away from her. I knew you'd be unable to resist lifting her skirts."

"I didn't lift her skirts."

"Oh? So you took her to the Nightingale to play back-gammon? How many times have you taken her there?"

He sighed in frustration. His relationship with Gina, what they'd done together was no one's business. Yet he knew speculation and gossip about them was already spreading throughout all of London. He was powerless to stop it and the scandal that would envelop her.

"Raising your voice, Rex, isn't going to help the situation," his father said quietly from where he stood, leaning against his desk. It might not help but it hurt far less than his father's disappointing tone. "The girl was under our protection, Andrew. Your actions are unconscionable."

"Don't be a hypocrite, Sterling," his mother chastised.

Andrew jerked his gaze to the woman who had born him. The look she was giving the Duke of Greystone spoke volumes.

"We weren't married when you first bedded me," she added succinctly.

Oh Lord, he didn't want to envision his father bedding his mother, did not want to know the intimate details of their lives. It seemed he was going to be punished for his actions regarding Gina in all manners imaginable.

"That was different, Frannie."

"In what way?"

Shifting uncomfortably, he crossed his arms over his chest. "It just was."

"Because I was a commoner, a bookkeeper, a woman with no prospects of marriage?"

"No, because I was irrevocably drawn to you."

She nodded, before turning her attention to Rex. "And you. Look me in the eye and swear to me that you did not have relations with Tillie before you wed her a few days ago."

"Of course I did. She was a divorcée, a woman with no reputation to protect. She was worldly, not an innocent like Gina."

"So you thought it perfectly all right to take advantage of her because her field had been plowed before?"

"No! Good God, I'm not having this conversation."

Andrew might have felt some sympathy for his brother if he wasn't so worried about Gina. He wanted to hold her, comfort her. Although it was entirely possible she'd want nothing else to do with him.

"You are," his mother said sternly. "Why did you bed her outside of marriage?"

"Because I was obsessed with her, but I don't see what that has to do with anything."

"You don't think it possible your brother shared the same obsession?"

He sighed. "I know he did. I saw the way he looked at her. That's the reason I warned him off." He glared at Andrew. "Why the bloody hell didn't you steer clear of her?"

"I believe, Rex," his mother said, "you've answered that question yourself. The why doesn't matter, but the girl's reputation is ruined and he will marry her."

"No," Andrew said forcefully, "I won't."

His mother looked at him as though she no longer recognized who he was. Disappointment filled her eyes as she slowly rose and walked over to him, her gaze scanning over his face as she searched for an answer she wasn't going to find. Never in his life had the success of a good bluff mattered so much. He had to give the impression Gina meant nothing to him, that his words weren't flaying his heart.

She stopped less than a yard away. "You compromised Gina."

"She is still a virgin."

"Do you think anyone is going to believe that when she was unmasked at that scandalous place? Why will you not marry her?"

"I may be the second son but I'm not going to be someone's second choice. I'm not going to be the one for whom someone settled. Marrying me will not make her a countess, or a marchioness, or a future duchess. It won't even give her the title of viscountess. She is in want of a title; she is deserving of one."

"No peer is going to marry her now," Rex said.

"I'll make it right. I'll speak with Somerdale. She fancies him. I'll explain it was a prank or a dare. I'll ensure he understands she is untouched."

"And why would he marry her?" his father asked.

"Because he has squandered a good bit of his inheritance and will soon be in need of the funds marriage to Gina will provide." And he was planning to ask for her hand anyway. She'd implied she would accept. Somerdale would need only a little nudging to look beyond the scandal.

"Does he love her?" his mother asked.

"I do not see how he cannot."

"What were you thinking?"

Gina sat on the bed, in her nightdress, with her back pressed against a mound of pillows. The duchess had insisted she bathe and then the woman had brushed her hair soothingly. Which, unfortunately, had caused Gina to burst into tears, remembering all the times her mother had brushed her hair when she was younger, before her mother died, and Tillie had stepped into the maternal role. "I wanted to see it. I thought it would be an adventure. And I know that after I marry, I will have to be a good and proper wife and not do things I ought not."

And she'd wickedly hoped that once there, Andrew would want to do more than just show her the place, that he would demonstrate exactly what transpired in the bed-chambers there. She'd planned to seduce him, completely and thoroughly. She'd been well on her way to having that happen. His eyes had reflected such desire, such longing.

"I thought my scandal was bad," Tillie said. "Yours will be so much worse if the rumors are not put to rest quickly. A hasty marriage is called for. Andrew will need to get a special license—"

"I'm not marrying him."

Tillie looked at her as though she'd gone mad. "Sweeting, you don't have a choice. No one is going to believe you are still an innocent."

"He has no wish to marry. He's made that abundantly clear, and while I don't agree with his reasoning, I must re-

spect his decision. I will not force him to marry me, nor will
I allow you or anyone else to force him. He would resent it,
and in time he would come to hate me."

Tillie sat on the edge of her bed and took her hands,
squeezed. "Gina, you'll not be welcomed into homes. Everyone will give you a cut direct. I've lived with that sort of
ostracism. It is not pleasant, dear sister. Even when you know
you are in the right, it can hurt unbearably."

"Then perhaps I shall return to New York."

"I thought you loved England."

"I do, but I have no fondness for being the object of scandal. On the other hand, neither do I relish the thought of
being chased away. I'm not certain what I'll do yet, but I do
know I shan't marry Andrew."

"On the one hand, I think you're being very admirable.
On the other, very foolish. Life for you is going to be quite
unpleasant, no matter how much I try to shield you."

"You don't have to shield me, Tillie. It was my idea to go
there. I'm fully capable of facing the repercussions on my
own."

Her sister gave her a sad smile. "When the deuce did you
grow up?"

Somewhere between a brothel and a house for assigna-
tions. Although she wasn't certain she'd matured as much as
she'd fallen in love.

CHAPTER 13

"Will you honor me by becoming my wife?"

Gina stared at Somerdale, kneeling before her in Rexton's front parlor, holding her hand, looking up at her imploringly. He'd arrived a half hour earlier to speak with Rexton in the library, and then he'd asked to speak with her alone. She'd had an inkling regarding what was coming. Still it was a shock.

"You are aware of the rumors circulating that I was spied at the Nightingale Club three nights ago."

"I am."

"And you are aware of the purpose behind the club's existence? Of what transpires within those walls?"

"I am, but Lord Andrew assures me nothing untoward happened between you, that you remain a virgin."

Andrew had spoken with him, disclosed those intimate details? He had gone to a man of whom he was obviously jealous and sought to convince him, on her behalf, that she was worthy of his hand in marriage. Why would he do that? "He did, did he?"

"Indeed. He was quite adamant regarding your untouched status. He waxed on quite poetically regarding your attributes and your suitability for becoming my countess."

"What exactly did he say?"

He furrowed his brow as though remembering were a difficult task. "That you are intelligent, witty, quick to learn, a delightful conversationalist, fascinating company—things I had, of course, discerned for myself. He said I would be the most fortunate man in all of England if you would agree to become my wife."

Blinking back the tears stinging her eyes, she could hardly fathom that Andrew had made such flattering claims regarding her. Was it possible he cared for her as much as she did him?

"And so here I am, willing to overlook the scandal that will surely keep all others from your door."

"How very generous of you, my lord." She hadn't seen Andrew since Tillie and Rexton had returned from Kingsbrook Park, but it wasn't the scandal keeping him away. She realized that with every fiber of her being. He stayed away because he hoped in doing so, she would acquire the marriage she had told him she desired. He was thinking of her, striving to ensure another led her to the altar.

"You are deserving of such generosity."

"According to Lord Andrew."

"Yes, well . . . according to my own observations as well. Still, I should like to wait a month before we make the announcement. Simply as a precaution." He cleared his throat. "So I am not made to look a fool."

Although she fully understood his caution, it still didn't sit well with her. She withdrew her hand from his. "You mean you wish to ensure I am not with child."

"Precisely."

"So you don't believe him."

He shoved himself to his feet. "I do, but still I see no harm in delaying the announcement."

The harm was that during those thirty days she would live with the scandal, the stares, and the speculations. Having him at her side without any formal declaration of an agreement between them would do little to quiet the gossips. As a matter of fact, it might only serve to increase the volume of their whispers.

But her face gave none of those thoughts away. If she'd learned anything at all during her time with Andrew, it was the value of a good bluff. She rose calmly and elegantly from the sofa. One step brought her nearer to him. Two allowed her to place her hand on his chest. "Forget all of Lord Andrew's compliments regarding me. Why do *you* want to marry me?"

His gaze dipped to her splayed fingers over his waistcoat. "Because I believe we are well suited."

She inched closer. "Do you desire me?"

"Do you doubt it?"

Yes, as a matter of fact she did. "Kiss me."

He glanced around as though searching for their audience.

"We are quite alone," she pointed out unnecessarily. Even the door was closed. Leaning toward him, she whispered, "Take possession of my lips. Do with them as you will."

His eyes widening, he fairly leaped beyond her reach. "You

are quite brazen, Miss Hammersley. It would be entirely inappropriate for me to take advantage when there is yet no official understanding between us."

Where was the passion, the hunger, the yearning? The *need* to taste, to touch, to possess? She marched forward; he staggered back. "You find me so easy to resist?"

"I am a gentleman, Miss Hammersley."

A boring one at that. He wouldn't take her to brothels or places where naughtiness occurred. He wouldn't snatch her into his arms because they felt empty without her there. He would make her a countess and she would make him a very wealthy man.

"The answer is no, my lord. While I appreciate your generous offer, it does not suit me." She spun on her heel and headed for the door.

"Lord Andrew assured me you would say yes."

Because Andrew was striving to rescue her once again. Only she was no longer in need of having another save her. She was fully capable of doing it herself. Stopping, she faced him. "Did he? Well, I do hope he didn't make any wagers on that outcome."

"I am your only hope to be saved from scandal."

For the first time in her life, she understood why her sister had risked so much in order to obtain a divorce from her first husband. "Please don't take offense, my lord, but I have discovered I'd rather live with scandal."

"I daresay you have a rather odd notion of what it entails in order to rescue me."

Gina was more than pleased with how abruptly Andrew looked up from the papers he was studying, how quickly he leaped to his feet with her proclamation when she strode into his library unannounced. "What the devil are you doing here?" He looked over her shoulder. "Did you come alone?"

"Yes, sans chaperone. A lady of scandal really doesn't have to bother with such nonsense."

"An unmarried lady does not come to a bachelor's residence unaccompanied."

"I would think a married one shouldn't either."

"A married woman already has a husband. She's not striving to lead a gent to the altar. She doesn't have to be quite as careful with her reputation. You, however—"

"I told him no." Casually she strolled farther into the room, taking additional delight in his obvious confusion. If his brow furrowed any more deeply he was likely to give himself a megrim.

"Somerdale? Why? I thought you fancied him."

She neared the desk, neared him. He made a hasty retreat to the fireplace, grabbed the mantel with one hand.

"You told me he was in debt."

"He's not completely insolvent. Your fortune will help him set matters to rights. He has a very fine estate, in need of a bit of upkeep, but you'll live comfortably there. And he has a London residence."

"You have a London residence."

"Mine is leased. His is owned."

He didn't back away when she got near enough to inhale his bergamot and lemony fragrance. But she noticed his knuckles were turning white with his grip of the mantel. "You encouraged him to ask for my hand. Why?"

"Because betrothal to him will go far in limiting the damage done by your discovery at the Nightingale. It makes it moot. It no longer matters. You are spoken for—after the incident. And people will get caught up in your betrothal— why did you dismiss him?"

Moving even closer, she pressed her palm against his chest. "Because his heart didn't pound against my fingertips. Because I didn't hear his breath hitch." She raised her gaze to his. "Because he didn't have to risk denting the marble of the mantel in order to stop himself from reaching for me. And it seemed wrong, so very wrong—" She lifted her hand to his jaw, resting her palm against the pulse at his throat, where it thrummed madly. "—to marry him when I loved another."

Ah, Christ. She did not mean him. She could not love him.

But it was there in the green of her eyes, in the intensity with which she looked at him, in the manner in which her fingers pressed against the underside of his jaw. And his pulse, damn it, responded as though she were pressing her mouth there, suckling and licking, and promising other things would be sucked and licked.

"Gina—"

"I know you have no wish to marry. I won't force you. I won't let your family force you. I'll be your lover, for as long as you'll have me. When you tire of me, I'll return to New York and live in a cottage by the sea."

His hand ached. He might have broken a bone, striving so hard to maintain a grip in order not to reach for her. Surrender had never felt so sweet as he released his hold on the mantel and cupped her cheek. "I *will* tire of you, you know."

Her chin came up a notch as she again nodded. "I know."

He stroked his thumb along the corner of her mouth. "I estimate, at the most, you would have only fifty or sixty years with me."

Her impish grin made his heart clench, his chest tighten painfully.

"I could live with that," she said quietly.

"That is a lot of years to live in sin. We should probably marry."

"I shall consider it, but only if you ask properly."

Only for her would Andrew do the one thing he'd never wanted to do, the one thing he'd never expected to do.

He dropped to one knee.

Taking her hand, he gently cradled it between both of his and held her gaze. "Miss Virginia Hammersley, as the second son I never wanted the title, the estates, or the responsibilities that came with being a peer. But for you, I'd willingly take on the burden of being a king so that you could be my queen."

"Andrew—"

"I adore you. I have from the moment I met you. If you will honor me by becoming my wife, I swear to you that I shall strive to do all in my power to ensure you never regret it."

Her smile was blinding. "What a fine match we make when I adore you as well. Yes, I'll marry you."

The joy and happiness that surged through him would
have brought him to his knees if he wasn't already there. He
shoved himself to his feet and kissed her, as tenderly and
gently as he could, forcing his desire for her into submis-
sion. He was mad for her and when she was this close, he
wanted her with an almost feral intensity. But until she was
his wife—*wife!* . . . a word he'd never thought to associate
with himself—he would keep himself on a taut tether.

Drawing back, he held her gaze. "I should probably
return you home so you can begin making plans. I don't want
to go too long without you in my bed."

"Actually." She moved in, pressed up against him, wound
her arms around his neck. "I am soon to take a husband, and
I was thinking I should like to experience one more adventure before I am shackled to him for life. An adventure between the sheets."

"Sweetheart, I held back once. I can't do it again."

"I don't want you to hold back." Raising up on her toes,
she nipped at his chin. "I want to be your lover before I'm
your wife."

With a low growl, he pressed his forehead to hers. "Damn
you. I shall never be able to resist giving you what you desire."

Then he lifted her into his arms and headed for the stairs.

CHAPTER 14

The swiftness with which their clothes became a heap on the floor once they reached his bedchamber should have startled her, but she was too eager to be with him to pay it much mind. It was thrilling to realize how desperately he wanted her, humbling to know how much determination it must have taken for him to resist the lure of her before now.

They landed on the bed in a tangle of arms, legs, and hungry mouths. They explored as though they'd never done so before, and yet the familiarity of his body made her feel as though she were coming home. She loved the bunching and tensing of his muscles beneath her fingers, loved the way his hands stroked and caressed her. His long arms could reach so much more of her than she could of him, but he seemed not to mind as his low groans and moans echoed around her.

She was going to become his wife, and she was left to wonder why she'd ever thought she wanted a titled gentleman. A title wasn't earned. It simply came with one's birth. What was earned was character, temperament, charm. Or at least it was part of a person that developed over time, that wasn't simply given.

She loved every aspect of Andrew. His fun nature, his willingness to take her on adventures that in all likelihood would lead to no good. While she had told him she wanted one more, this one with him now, she had no intention of not asking for more later. Once they were married, once they were husband and wife.

He skimmed his fingers over her hip, along her inner thigh, bringing them to rest at the very heart of her core. "What word did Venus teach you for this?"

She wrinkled her nose. "Cunny. Notch. But I don't like them. Teach me another."

"Paradise." He held her gaze. "You're wet and ready for me. Are you sure, sweetheart?"

"I've never been more sure of anything."

He captured her mouth. She felt him nudging at her opening. Raising her knees, tilting her hips up, she welcomed him. As he pushed in, the discomfort was slight. She dug her fingers into his shoulders as her body stretched to accommodate him.

When he was seated to the hilt, he emitted a low growl. "You feel so damned good."

"So do you."

He chuckled. "We're both going to feel a good deal better when we're done here."

He withdrew slightly, thrust forward. Again and again. She met his thrusts, taking him deep, swelling with satisfaction. The tempo increased, the sensations built, radiating out from her core, causing her toes and fingers to tingle. He suckled at her breast, pressed kisses to her neck, once more claimed her mouth.

Intertwining their fingers, he held her hands over her head, pumping into her with a fevered pitch. The passion escalated, the ecstasy blossomed and bloomed—

Her resounding cry was matched with his harsh groan as pleasure engulfed both of them. When they went still, with their harsh breathing echoing around them, she wondered how it was that they'd both managed to survive.

Slowly, lethargically, he rolled off her and brought her up close against his side.

"Are you all right?" he asked.

"More than all right." Giggling, she hugged him. "That was marvelous."

"You were marvelous."

Lifting up slightly, she met his gaze. "You will be happy being married, I promise."

"Married, not married, whenever I'm with you I'm happy."

She nipped at his chin. "That's not true. You've been put out with me on several occasions."

"I still enjoyed those occasions."

"I love you, Andrew."

Threading his fingers through her hair, he brought her lips down to his, kissing her as though he could not have enough of her. She was surprised that so soon after, he could already stir her passions back to life.

Nudging her gently, he guided her until she was straddling him. Reaching back, she wrapped her hands around his erection. "Mmm. I didn't think you wanted to settle for porridge, my lord."

"That was before I remembered it could be served with sugar, or currants, or milk or cream. That it need not always be the same. That was before I fell deeply and madly in love with you."

EPILOGUE

From the Journal of Lord Andrew Mabry

With the announcement of our betrothal, the scandal quickly faded, replaced by the shock that an American heiress was actually on the verge of leading me—a man who had sworn to never marry—to the altar. Gina soon found herself inundated with visitors, young ladies who wanted to learn her secret for convincing a marriage-shy lord to embrace the bonds of holy matrimony. Apparently I wasn't the only lord reluctant to be shackled.

I'm not certain what advice she dished out. Had they inquired of me, I'd have told them it was quite simple really: give him cause to fall madly in love with you.

I'm not exactly certain when I did fall in love with her—or even when I realized that I had. I don't think in either case it was a single moment but rather an accumulation of smiles, laughter, conversation, and adventures. It's an odd thing but I can no longer remember a time when I didn't love her.

We married on a Tuesday with church bells pealing and people issuing congratulations. Tillie gifted us with Landsdowne Court and so we made it our home, although we also spent considerable time at the family estates.

From the moment Gina's mother brought her to England, she was certain she would marry a titled gentleman, would become a countess or a duchess. Instead she married the spare.

I, for one, could not have been more grateful. We lived an active and exciting life, filled with travel and challenges. Adventures of all sorts. While her inheritance saw us well cared for and ensured we never had to worry over money, that we could in fact play all we wanted, we turned our energies toward more lasting endeavors.

Gina was a leader in the women's suffrage movement, while I served in the House of Commons. Together, through a lengthy process and many years, we worked to ensure women had the right to vote. It was with a great deal of pride that we watched our daughters and nieces vote for the first time.

We had a good life, Gina and I. A very good life indeed, during which we enjoyed an amazing amount of porridge.

Coming soon from *New York Times*
bestselling author Lorraine Heath,
the first in a breathtaking new series

BEYOND SCANDAL AND DESIRE

At birth, Mick Trewlove, the illegitimate son of a duke, was handed over to a commoner. Despite his lowly upbringing, Mick has become a successful businessman, but all his wealth hasn't satisfied his need for revenge against the man who still won't acknowledge him. What else can Mick do but destroy the duke's *legitimate* son—and woo the heir's betrothed into his own unloving arms . . .

Orphaned and sheltered, Lady Aslyn Hastings longs for a bit of adventure. With her intended often preoccupied, Aslyn finds herself drawn to a darkly handsome entrepreneur who seems to understand her so well. Surely a lady of her station should avoid Mick Trewlove. If only he weren't so irresistible . . .

As secrets are about to be exposed, Mick must decide if his plan for vengeance is worth risking what his heart truly desires.

LORRAINE HEATH always dreamed of being a writer. After graduating from the University of Texas, she wrote training manuals, press releases, articles, and computer code, but something was always missing. When she read a romance novel, she not only became hooked on the genre, but quickly realized what her writing lacked: rebels, scoundrels, and rogues. She's been writing about them ever since. Her work has been recognized with numerous industry awards, including RWA's prestigious RITA®. Her novels have appeared on the *USA Today* and *New York Times* bestseller lists.

Discover great authors, exclusive offers, and more at hc.com.

A LETTER FROM THE EDITOR

Dear Reader,

I hope you liked the latest romance from Avon Impulse! If you're looking for another steamy, fun, emotional read, be sure to check out some of our upcoming titles.

First up we have a delightful new story compilation from superstar Eloisa James! *A MIDSUMMER NIGHT'S DISGRACE AND OTHER STORIES* includes a short but sweet dip into the world of her beloved Essex Sisters, as well as other Cinderella-themed novellas! Eloisa always delivers a witty, charming read and this collection is no different!

We also have a brand-new series from Mia Sosa for all you contemporary romance fans! Mia makes her Avon Impulse debut with *ACTING ON IMPULSE*, a fun, flirty (and a little dirty) novel about a Hollywood heartthrob who meets the woman of his dreams on an airplane . . . except she doesn't recognize him! Sparks may fly, but what will happen when she finds out the truth? You'll have to read this sexy, diverse romantic comedy to find out!

You can purchase any of these titles by clicking the links above or by visiting our website, www.AvonRomance.com. Thank you for loving romance as much as we do . . . enjoy!

Sincerely,

Nicole Fischer

Editorial Director

Avon Impulse